GOOD & EVIL

Lacey Deaver

Published by
World Video Bible School®
25 Lantana Lane
Maxwell, Texas 78656
www.wvbs.org

Copyright 2014 WVBS

ISBN: 9780989431163

Cover art by Ethan Deaver

Layout by Aubrie Deaver

Serving the Church since 1986

wvbs.org

The Story:

This Christian-fiction story was provided by my grandfather, Rudy Cain, who used biblical principles to tell this story.

Dedicated To:
My loving parents, Weylan and Cheri Deaver,
for always supporting and encouraging me in my
desire to write.
I love you both so much!

I hope you enjoy reading this book, and that
God will receive all the glory!

Lacey Deaver

TABLE OF CONTENTS

"And war broke out in heaven: Michael and his angels fought with the dragon; and the dragon and his angels fought, but they did not prevail, nor was a place found for them in heaven any longer. So the great dragon was cast out, that serpent of old, called the Devil and Satan, who deceives the whole world; he was cast to the earth, and his angels were cast out with him."   *-Revelation 12:7-9*

"For if God did not spare the angels who sinned, but cast them down to hell and delivered them into chains of darkness, to be reserved for judgment; and did not spare the ancient world, but saved Noah, one of eight people, a preacher of righteousness, bringing in the flood on the world of the ungodly; and turning the cities of Sodom and Gomorrah into ashes, condemned them to destruction, making them an example to those who afterward would live ungodly;"   *-2 Peter 2:4-6*

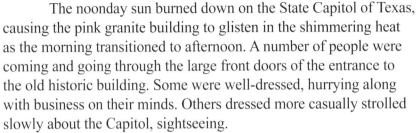

The noonday sun burned down on the State Capitol of Texas, causing the pink granite building to glisten in the shimmering heat as the morning transitioned to afternoon. A number of people were coming and going through the large front doors of the entrance to the old historic building. Some were well-dressed, hurrying along with business on their minds. Others dressed more casually strolled slowly about the Capitol, sightseeing.

Leaving from a door that led to the Senate offices was a young man in his late twenties, with his light blond hair parted on the side and combed carefully back from his forehead. He was sharply dressed in a dark suit and carried a briefcase in his left hand. He looked very professional and put together, but the discouraged and concerned expression on his face betrayed his well-appointed attire and spoke to the urgent thoughts that were gnawing at him. Worry clouded Keith Davidson's mind as he walked briskly down the steps of the Capitol building and through the front gates onto Congress Street, the thoroughfare of Austin.

As Keith made his way along the wide, busy street past rows of banks, offices, and commerce buildings, he could smell the enticing aroma of food coming from the small restaurants tucked away between the skyscrapers. The scent of barbecue and Chinese food made his mouth water, reminding Keith of the meal he had shared with his wife and son the night before at a barbecue in their back yard. Keith's stomach growled. He checked his watch. Both hands pointed to noon, but he dared not stop for lunch. He was so hungry that even the hot dog stand on the corner looked tempting. But Keith couldn't afford to stop. He knew he had to get back to the office as quickly as he could.

When he reached the corner of Congress and 6th Street, Keith stopped in front of an especially tall building that towered into the Texas sky. On the front of the building in large lettering read Congress 601. Keith stood there in the burning heat looking

GOOD & EVIL

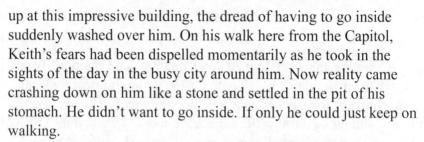

up at this impressive building, the dread of having to go inside suddenly washed over him. On his walk here from the Capitol, Keith's fears had been dispelled momentarily as he took in the sights of the day in the busy city around him. Now reality came crashing down on him like a stone and settled in the pit of his stomach. He didn't want to go inside. If only he could just keep on walking.

But Keith couldn't stand there on the sidewalk forever. The sun beat down mercilessly upon his head and shoulders, and the young man felt suddenly as parched as if he were lost in a desert. He exhaled loudly, gripped the smooth metal handle bar on one of the large glass doors, pulled it open, and let himself into the building. As he entered the busy foyer, he passed the office directory on his way to the pair of elevators. As he glanced at the directory out of habit, Keith's eye was drawn to the 37th floor designation that read Krantz Properties. Keith always noticed that single entry. He rarely looked at any of the others. He got into one of the elevators and pressed the button for the 37th floor.

Standing in the elevator, the trip up to his designated floor seemed agonizingly slow for Keith as he began thinking over what he was going to say to his boss, knowing the report he had to give was sure to be unwelcome to his employer. Keith's fear escalated as the elevator continued to ascend. Various people who also worked in the building got on and off the elevator as it made its way up, but Keith didn't talk to any of them. He stood back in the corner of the elevator, moving his lips silently as he rehearsed in his mind the information he would very shortly have to report.

With a cheerful *"ding"* the elevator doors opened on the 37th floor. Keith was the only occupant in the elevator by the time he reached his destination, and stepped out onto the quiet hall. He walked over to the drinking fountain near the elevators, his mouth dry with worry, and after his drink straightened up, wiping his lips. Adjusting his tie with a resigned look on his face, he headed toward the double glass doors and walked through them, passing a sign on his right that said "Krantz Properties Inc." Keith was well aware as he glanced at the sign that the entire 37th floor was taken up by Mr. Krantz's empire – mainly his real estate business – and the other businesses he owned.

Keith entered the main lobby outside the office, where he said good afternoon to the receptionist behind her desk. The pretty young Asian woman was on the phone but acknowledged Keith's greeting with a smile and a wave. Then he walked through a second door into a smaller yet still luxurious room – the office of Mr. Krantz's personal secretary. A kind-looking woman in her mid-thirties with long brown hair pinned up in a bun, she wore a silver blouse and dark skirt and was typing on the computer at her desk. As Keith walked in the secretary looked up and gave him a quick smile of recognition before resuming her work.

Keith walked up to the secretary's desk, inwardly nervous but trying to maintain his outward composure.

"Mrs. Miller, I need to see Mr. Krantz."

Judith Miller looked up from her computer screen. She glanced over at the button on the phone which indicated whether or not Mr. Krantz was on a call. The small light glowed bright green.

"He's on the phone, Keith. You'll have to wait. I don't think he'll be long. Can I get you something to drink?"

Keith sat down in one of the two chairs near the secretary's desk, the agony of anticipation starting to creep over him again. He barely heard Judith's question.

"Oh...no thanks, Mrs. Miller," he said, staring vacantly out the big window with the view toward the Capitol, reminding him once again of the report he was going to have to make in person to the man in the other office. Keith always hated admitting he had failed at something, especially to his superior, and today was no exception. What would Mr. Krantz say?

Keith tried to sit still in the chair while he waited, but butterflies filled his stomach, and when he clasped his hands together between his knees in an effort to hold himself together, he found that his palms were sweaty. To distract himself, he looked around the office, trying to lose his thoughts in the details of the furnishings.

He had been an intern at Krantz Properties for just over a year, so he knew his way around the building and was familiar with the business, but every time he stepped onto the 37th floor he was struck by its splendor. Even the private secretary's office was furnished to reflect the success of the business. The two adjacent desks were made of an expensive dark wood that was polished to a shine. There was a thick, soft carpet on the floor and in the corners nearest to the desks were two potted plants, their leafy tendrils green and lush. Along the walls hung a few tasteful paintings, but most of the pictures hanging up were those of properties Mr. Krantz owned: industrial tracts, office buildings, malls, and international resort properties. As Keith studied these pictures he couldn't help but be impressed by the great success of his boss.

His boss...who he knew was not going to be happy with him after what Keith had to tell him. The young man's heart started pounding harder again.

Okay, I need to distract myself or I'll be a nervous wreck, then it will be even worse, thought Keith desperately. He looked up at Judith Miller, who was still typing quietly away on her computer.

"Mrs. Miller?"

"Yes?"

"How long have you been working for Mr. Krantz?"

Judith's eyes never left the screen. "Almost three years."

Keith nodded. He had graduated from the University of Texas in Austin with a Bachelor's degree and had taken the intern job to feed his small family. He was looking for a job with a greater potential for career growth, but since good jobs were hard to come by these days, he had taken what he could get to support his wife and son.

"I've only been here for a year," he commented, just to keep up the conversation. "I can't imagine how you've put up with this place as long as you have."

The typing stopped. Judith Miller sighed. She looked at Keith over the top of her computer screen. "You do what you have to when you have a sick child and mother to support," she replied soberly. She turned to look at the credenza on her right, which held several framed pictures of a smiling little boy. Keith looked at the pictures and remembered.

"How *is* your son?" he asked.

She sighed again, a soft, sorrowful sound. "Since the operation his prognosis has improved. But the doctors seem to think it will take a long while for him to recover."

She resumed typing and Keith was left sitting in a more despondent state than before. Then a new thought occurred to him. A question that had been nagging at the back of his mind since he started working at Krantz Properties rose to his lips.

"Mrs. Miller, is it true that Mr. Krantz had a partner, and wasn't that partner the one who started this whole company in the first place?"

"Yes, Keith."

"And didn't that partner's wife work here in the office also?" he asked without looking up.

"Yes, that's what I understand," Judith answered calmly.

"I also heard she had an affair with the boss, and the whole thing got out of hand with a drug overdose and an attempted suicide," Keith said, this time turning his head to see the secretary's reaction. She looked back at him steadily.

"Keith, I can't talk about that," she said firmly, but with bitterness in her voice as she glanced toward Mr. Krantz's office door on her right. "First of all, it wouldn't be right," she continued, "and secondly, all I can tell you is that there is no partner now."

Keith's eyebrows narrowed as he digested the information. "What happened to the partner's wife?" he asked. "Did she die? I heard someone in the office say she was dead."

Judith shook her head.

"All I know now is that she was in a treatment center in California," the secretary replied quietly, glancing once more at the formidable door of her boss. She looked down at her keyboard again, and noticed the glowing green phone light that connected to her office had now turned off.

"Mr. Krantz is off the phone now. I will let him know you're here," she said, glad to be done with the conversation. She stood up and walked out from behind the desk.

Keith slowly rose. "Okay, but he isn't going to want to see me," he muttered, following Judith Miller towards Mr. Krantz's door. He stopped a few feet behind her and waited nervously as the secretary knocked softly at the door.

"Yes?"

The voice from inside was dark and sounded irritated.

Uh oh, thought Keith. *He's already in a bad mood. Wonderful.*

Judith opened the door and timidly stepped into the doorway of the large office. Behind a huge desk in the corner of the room a man sat in a large leather swivel chair examining financial spreadsheets. He barely looked up at his secretary.

"Come in Judith," he said in a long-suffering voice, as if he had been interrupted during the most important job in the world but was being forced to sacrifice his precious time.

Judith walked hastily forward, her voice thin and nervous when she spoke.

"Mr. Krantz, I'm sorry to disturb you but one of our interns, Keith Davidson, is waiting in my office to see you."

Mr. Krantz quickly raised his eyes. Judith tried to mask her dislike as she gazed into their inky depths beneath the masterful black brows.

"Yes, Judith. Send him in."

Jack Krantz was not feigning disinterest now. He turned over the spreadsheets on his desk so they could not be read. Then he stood up and walked to the large office window where he could see the Capitol Building standing in the distance. With one arm behind his back and the other hand in his pocket, Jack smirked at his own clear-cut reflection in the streak-free glass, anticipating

CHAPTER 1: THE NERVOUS INTERN

the good news he expected to hear from his intern in the next few moments.

The secretary had gone back into her office and motioned Keith to go into the next room.

"Mr. Krantz will see you now, Keith."

"Thanks, Judith. Wish me luck," he murmured. Judith gave Keith a sympathetic look as he passed by her, and she pulled the door closed behind him.

"Let no one say when he is tempted, 'I am tempted by God'; for God cannot be tempted by evil, nor does He Himself tempt anyone. But each one is tempted when he is drawn away by his own desires and enticed. Then, when desire has conceived, it gives birth to sin; and sin, when it is full-grown, brings forth death."   **-James 1:13-15**

Keith stood silently inside the spacious office, trying to steady his nerves. It was one of the largest offices he had ever seen. The two walls opposite the door were actually two giant windows, offering a spectacular view of the great city of Austin with the Capitol Building towering majestically among the skyscrapers.

The massive mahogany desk was angled to face the door in front of the windows. Heavy leather chairs in front of the desk were separated by a glass table. In the center of the table stood a large bronze sculpture of a cowboy on a rearing horse. The rope in the bronze figure's hand was pulled taut around the neck of a longhorn steer, its mouth open in a silent bawl. To the right of Mr. Krantz's desk sat a large, inlaid world globe.

Even the walls of Mr. Krantz's office boasted of the businessman's achievements. A couple of plaques from Texas A&M University adorned the walls, along with several framed business diplomas, that intermingled with pictures of motivational sayings and scenes that expressed the go-getter attitude of Mr. Krantz and his policy regarding the way he did business. The pictures, plaques and diplomas halted in their march along the walls to make room for a large plasma-screen TV. The news was on with the volume turned down very low. Behind the desk a dark credenza completely filled the corner where the two window-walls met. The credenza held two large computer monitors and keyboards.

The dark, strategically placed furniture that decorated the office was arranged to create an illusion of power, strength, and success. It was a place designed to make a businessman either feel at home or intimidated.

Jack Krantz remained standing behind his desk in front of the window with his back to Keith when the young man entered his office. Jack did not turn to greet him when he came in, but Keith could see his boss's reflection in the window pane.

Jack Krantz was a well-built man. At forty years of age

he was in good physical condition, as it was his habit to work out four or five times a week. He had very dark hair with a streak of gray here and there, combed back perfectly from his forehead with every single strand in place. He had a pale, thin face with heavy black brows above his calculating, black eyes. His hard face and the stern slant of his mouth commanded an authoritative presence, as one has when accustomed to being obeyed. He could be pleasant enough when he was in a good mood, but his temper was like a deadly serpent when aroused.

Keith saw in Jack's reflection that Jack was wearing a confident smile, and the intern's dread deepened.

"So, Keith," Jack began genially, "you made your first big deal, eh?"

Jack had still not turned to face him. Keith walked slowly toward the center of the room, wishing he didn't have to report what he knew he had to. He took a deep breath.

The intern's nervous silence roused Jack's curiosity and impatience.

"Well, Keith?" he said expectantly, still without looking around. He only turned his head slightly to the side.

Jack's deep, dark voice hung heavily around Keith's ears, and for a minute he almost lost his nerve. One word from Jack Krantz was enough to quench any courage one might have, especially if one knew he was about to be the source of oncoming anger from the man.

Keith licked his dry lips.

"Well sir, I'm afraid I've got some bad news. I..."

He paused because he could tell Jack's countenance had changed. In his reflection in the window his confident smirk had faded to a menacing scowl.

"What is the problem, Keith?" he growled, feeling his impatience ripening to irritation.

"I...I...I didn't...I couldn't..." Keith tried to say, but stopped suddenly as Jack whirled around to face him.

Jack Krantz strode fiercely around his desk and across

the big room to where the young intern now stood. When he saw the viciousness in his boss's face, Keith could barely keep from turning around and running for the door. When Jack stood almost directly in front of Keith, Keith wasn't sure if Jack was going to strike him or not. However, the intern stood his ground, clamping his fists tightly against his sides. He was noticeably shaken as he looked into the cold, dark eyes of his boss who was almost face to face with him.

"You didn't *what?* You couldn't *what?*" Jack's voice was a burning hiss. "Boy, don't you tell me what you can't do," Jack growled, looking Keith squarely in the eyes. "Just what do you mean by you 'couldn't'?"

Keith jumped at the angry rise in Jack's voice.

"I wasn't able to convince Senator Watson to take the money, sir. In fact, he wouldn't even talk to me about his vote on the land-use bill," Keith blurted out, trembling.

Jack put his fists on his hips, seething. His black eyes narrowed to slits as he held Keith's gaze.

"What do you mean he *wouldn't?*" said Jack in a dangerous voice. "Your job was to convince him to take the money and to vote the way we told him. A simple job, Keith. I wouldn't have thought even you could botch this one."

"I tried, Mr. Krantz. I really tried!" the intern pleaded. "But he just wouldn't listen to anything I had to say!"

Jack closed his eyes as if asking himself how long he would have to put up with such incompetence.

"Keith, you are completely worthless," he said calmly, opening his eyes again. "But I suppose that's what I deserve for sending a boy to do a man's job."

Keith hung his head under the stinging words. "But Mr. Krantz, I–"

"No! No 'buts', Keith. Really, what's so hard about giving a senator an envelope full of money? I don't want excuses. I want *results!* I don't accept anything else."

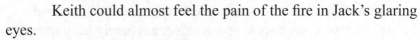

Keith could almost feel the pain of the fire in Jack's glaring eyes.

"You get back up to the Capitol building – *now* – and get Senator Watson's vote – *any way you can*," Jack told the intern. "Whatever it takes, do it. Do you understand me?"

Keith realized his hands were shaking, and he quickly put them in his pockets.

"But how will I even get him to talk to me?" he mumbled, almost afraid to ask.

Jack gave him an exasperated look and walked back behind his desk, gesturing for Keith to come forward. Crouching down he unlocked a door in the lower half of the credenza. Behind the door was a safe which Jack used a combination to open. Looking in briefly, he took out an envelope and glanced inside it. Nodding in satisfaction, he closed the envelope and tossed it carelessly in Keith's direction. The intern caught it as it slid across the desk, glanced at it and then at Jack, his gaze questioning.

"I've kept this picture of Senator Watson for such a purpose as this," Jack said casually to Keith. "When he sees this, I have no doubt that he'll talk to you."

Keith looked down at the envelope. With a glance at his boss, who nodded his permission, Keith slid a photo part way out of the envelope. A look of disgust spread over his face, and he quickly shoved the picture back inside. Krantz's lips twisted upward in a cold smile.

"Mr. Krantz, do you *really* want me to do this?" Keith pleaded. Blackmail was not something he wanted to be a party to.

Jack cocked his head and studied the young man as if trying to decide what to do with him.

"Keith, if you want to work one more day for me or for anyone else in this state, you better get this done today and report back here when you have it taken care of."

Keith could not miss the open threat in his boss's words. Slowly he put the envelope in his coat pocket, hanging his head like a beaten dog before its master.

"Now, get out of here and go do the job right this time," Jack said, turning his back to Keith again. The young man turned and left the office, closing the door behind himself without another word.

As the door to his office closed, Jack Krantz walked over to the window which afforded the spectacular view of the city. Standing in his habitual pose with one arm behind his back and the other resting against the window frame, Jack gazed out at the Capitol building that loomed high in the distance. Then he walked back to his desk and buzzed his secretary on the intercom.

"Judith, has the law office delivered the paperwork I requested for today?" he asked.

"Yes sir," Judith's voice came over the speaker. "It's just arrived. Shall I send someone to serve the papers?"

"No," Jack responded quickly. In spite of his anger and annoyance with Keith, a small half smile crept onto his face. "I'll be right out."

Jack picked up his coat and left his office. He walked over to Judith's desk and the secretary placed an envelope in his hand.

Jack opened the envelope and checked the papers inside.

"I'll take care of this myself," he told Judith. Then as he turned away he whispered to himself, "And I'm going to enjoy every minute of it. Here's one thing at least that's going to brighten up my lousy day."

With another cruel smile he walked toward the door, then stopped. Turning around, he went back to his secretary's desk.

"When Keith returns, I want you to fire him," Jack said to Judith. Her eyes grew wide with astonishment. "Tell him to clean out his desk before the end of the day," Jack continued. "Do you understand, Judith?"

"But, but Mr. Krantz, it wouldn't be right for *me* to fire him!" Judith spluttered anxiously. She had always thought Keith was a nice person and didn't want to be the one to tell him he had lost his job.

Jack furrowed his dark brow in annoyance. He fixed his

13

piercing gaze on the secretary and said very slowly, "You fire him before I get back or I'll have you cleaning out your desk as well."

Judith trembled and nodded once, looking down at her desk.

"Yes, sir," she mumbled.

Jack, still angry about Keith's incompetence and now on top of that, his secretary was reluctant to do his dirty work. He strode to the door and put his hand out to push it open. Suddenly he rounded on Judith.

"And speaking of firing, the next time you are late to work, you can kiss this job goodbye—sick kid or not," he snarled pitilessly. "You single mothers are always whining about a sick kid or giving some other flimsy excuse to come in late. And another thing, the next time you come crying into my office asking for time off to visit your mother – cancer or not – will be the last day you work for me!"

With those final threats, Jack Krantz yanked the door open and slammed it behind him. Back at her desk Judith Miller put her head in her hands and sobbed.

In the parking garage Jack walked briskly to his sleek, Nero Pastello Ferrari 458 Italia and slid into the plush, leather seat surrounded by exquisite interior, and starting the engine with a roar that made him smile when the eight-cylinder engine came to life. Driving his car always made him feel powerful and important. As he drove through the busy streets of the city, he passed the Capitol where Jack assumed his soon-to-be-fired intern was taking care of business. Jack shook his head as he thought about Keith.

Kid has a heart of cheese and lack of motivation to boot, he thought irritably. *It's a wonder he can hold down a job for a week. Always complaining or questioning what I need him to do. I give him a simple job and what does he do? He muffs it. And then he gets wishy-washy over using the leverage. He won't be getting any recommendation from me. I doubt he could ever make it up the corporate ladder anyway.*

Jack smiled tightly and drummed his fingers against the steering wheel.

And that Judith Miller...

Should he fire her too? Jack idly debated with himself for a moment.

No...at least not yet. A secretary who jumps at your every move is hard to come by right now, he thought. *Sure, she's annoying with all that yammer about sick family members, but she'll work for low wages without question. Desperation comes in handy when you want someone to work more for less pay. I'll leave her alone for now.*

With these thoughts Jack drove on until he was in a less populated part of the city, then took a ramp onto the interstate. After about fifteen minutes he took an exit off the interstate and was soon driving past crop fields with houses scattered farther apart. Jack pulled off onto a gravel lane that ran parallel between sun-warmed cotton fields.

When he rounded a bend in the road, Jack could see the old wood-framed house which was his destination. The small house was the only place for what looked like miles around, aside from a few dilapidated outbuildings surrounding it. There was also an old barn with a rusty wire pen containing a diminutive number of scraggly chickens. Besides these few buildings and the cotton fields, nothing but flat land stretched away from the house as far as the eye could see. The house was situated on at least several hundred acres of ground. As he drove closer and closer it became easier to see the state of disrepair the old house had fallen into. The building looked like it dated back to the late 1940's, with a metal roof discolored by time and worn with rust. It had a large front porch with old wooden steps in danger of rotting through. On the left side of the porch was a ramp about six steps high. The only area around the house that exemplified beauty was the small but well-kept flower garden to the right of the porch beneath three front windows. A few yards from the front porch a large oak tree rose tall and majestic, providing shade over the crumbling buildings and sun-baked earth.

As Jack pulled up close to the house and parked his car, a young woman straightened up from where she was working in the flower bed. Leaning on the garden rake in her hand, she watched the shiny black sports car come to a stop in front of the house. When she saw who stepped out of it, her eyes narrowed.

Jack closed the door of his car with casual ease and began walking toward the house. He took no notice of the woman until, as he put his foot on the first porch step, a voice behind him suddenly arrested his attention.

"Jack Krantz!"

The voice was high and filled with anger. Jack let out a little sigh of annoyance and slowly turned around.

The young woman stood before him, her jeans dirty from kneeling in the soil. Her shirt was damp from the heat and she was still holding the garden rake. Here and there her red hair was coming out of its long braid. Her face however, with those brilliant blue eyes and sweet mouth, was very attractive and usually gave her a continual expression of kindness. Now, however, the eyes were blazing and the mouth was trembling in rage.

"You've got some nerve showing up here," she said furiously to Jack. "You aren't welcome in this house. Get off our property – *now!*"

Jack rolled his eyes during her speech and folded his arms.

"Oh, it's you," he said scathingly, as if the woman were some irritating object in his way. "Still trying to protect that worthless brother of yours, are you?" He scoffed. "What a pitiful existence..."

The woman's mouth opened to speak, but he cut her off.

"Oh, and by the way, you can't order me off this land. It's not yours to begin with," he added.

"No, but it's my brother's land!" she cried, pushing a few strands of her bright red hair out of her face as she spoke.

Jack Krantz laughed coldly. "Wrong, sister. Want to try again?"

The woman looked confused. Then she advanced a few steps toward him, her fury mounting.

"What do you mean by that?" she demanded, clutching the long, sharp four-pronged garden rake so hard that her knuckles were turning white. Unconsciously she raised the rake in both hands in a defensive stance. Jack, not intimidated by her at all, looked down at the rake and snickered. "Are you going to use that for something?" he demanded, his eyes full of condescension. The young woman looked down at the rake in her hands, shook her head slightly and set it against the porch railing. Then she folded her arms, still glaring at Jack.

"What are you doing here?" she demanded.

Jack tucked his sunglasses into his coat pocket.

"I'm here to see Tyler," he answered. "Where is he?"

The young woman's eyes narrowed to slits again, and her mouth shrank to a thin line.

"He's in the house. But he won't see you! I can tell you that for sure," she said as Jack turned away from her to walk up the porch steps.

"Oh, he's going to see me," Jack said, walking up the steps. The woman quickly darted around him and stood in front of him on the porch, blocking his path to the door. Jack was forced to stop.

"You're not welcome here," she repeated acidly. "Leave."

Jack rolled his eyes again. Who did this girl think she was to try and stop him from getting what he wanted?

"Welcome or not, I'm going to see that sorry brother of yours," he informed her in a commanding voice. "We have business to attend to so, if you please, Miss Emerson..."

With that, Jack deftly pushed the young woman out of his way and opened the front door. Elizabeth Emerson gasped with indignation and rushed after Jack into the house.

"Repay no one evil for evil. Have regard for good things in the sight of all men. If it is possible, as much as depends on you, live peaceably with all men. Beloved, do not avenge yourselves, but rather give place to wrath; for it is written, 'Vengeance is Mine, I will repay,' says the Lord. Therefore'If your enemy is hungry, feed him; If he is thirsty, give him a drink;For in so doing you will heap coals of fire on his head.' Do not be overcome by evil, but overcome evil with good."   **-Romans 12:17-21**

CHAPTER 3: THE EMERSONS

Jack opened the screen door and stood on the threshold, looking around with a mixed expression of distaste and arrogance as he surveyed the small living room. Two shabby chairs, a worn couch, a small side table, and a medium-sized television made up the furniture in the room. A few old pictures adorned the pale walls, and dark blue curtains were pushed back from the windows to let in the light. The humble room was neat and clean, but by far not up to the businessman's standards.

He sniffed, and Elizabeth, coming in behind him, gave him an icy look.

Jack raised his voice. "Where are you, Tyler? You and I need to talk."

There was a slight creaking noise and from a doorway to the right a man in a wheelchair appeared, wheeling himself into the living room under the gaze of the two standing there.

Tyler Emerson was only in his mid-thirties, but the weariness in his eyes and the sorrowful patience in his expression gave his chiseled, handsome face more years than he had experienced. His light hair was carefully combed, and he was neatly dressed in jeans and a plaid shirt. When he saw Jack Krantz his eyes widened in surprise. In response, Jack sneered.

Before he could say anything however, Elizabeth pushed past him and went to stand beside her brother.

"Tyler, I told him he wasn't welcome here, and I told him to leave. Don't talk to him. He has no business being here, especially after the way he's treated you," she said, glaring at Jack as she spoke.

Tyler put his hand on his sister's arm.

"Lizzie, it's okay," he told her gently. "Jack has driven all the way out here. The least we can do is give him the courtesy of hearing what he has to say."

19

Elizabeth stared at him in astonishment. But seeing Tyler was in earnest she backed away and stood silently with her arms folded, still glaring at Jack.

"So, Jack," Tyler began, wheeling himself forward a little more. "What's so important that it could pull you away from your office in the middle of the day and bring you out here?"

Tyler's voice was calm and courteous, but Jack ignored the question.

"Tyler, take a long, hard look around you," he said, spreading his arms to indicate the surrounding area. "What do you see? You're living in a dump. You're practically penniless. You're a cripple who is confined to a wheelchair–"

"That's enough!" Elizabeth suddenly burst out, breaking into Jack's revilement. "You can't talk to my brother like that!"

Jack didn't even look at her, but kept speaking as though he hadn't been interrupted.

"You're living with your guard dog of a sister," he continued as he maintained eye contact with Tyler, well aware of Elizabeth writhing in anger out of the corner of his eye. "You have no job. You have no friends. And nothing is ever going to change any of that..."

Jack's eyes narrowed as he looked at the man in the wheelchair before him. He shook his head with a derisive scoff.

"You're a pathetic excuse for a man." he said.

Jack's words hurled themselves at Tyler like a storm of bullets. Throughout the onslaught the crippled man sat silently, keeping his eyes fixed on Jack's, but it was hard to hide the pain in his eyes from the cruel lash of words.

"How dare you speak to him like that!" Elizabeth broke in again, her pretty face pale as concern for her brother and fury toward Jack chased each other across her face while she looked from one man to the other.

"*You* are the cause of all this misery!" she cried, pointing an accusing finger at Jack. "From the moment Tyler became your partner, he's had nothing but trouble in his life. You are the reason

Tyler is sitting in that chair! It's because of you he can't even stand up on his own! And you stole his wife–"

Jack immediately put up a hand to stop her.

"Don't try to throw *that* in my face!" he said, his voice sounding a warning. "I didn't 'steal' Rachel. She left Tyler and married me of her own free will. No one forced her to. She just wanted to be with a *real* man."

"And what did it get her?" Elizabeth demanded furiously. "Rachel was a good wife and a good mother before you came along and led her astray. Tyler is ten times the man you will ever be– "

"Jack," Tyler interrupted suddenly, "I don't know where Rachel is. I'm very worried about her. Can you help me contact her? I want to help her. Do you know where she might be?"

Jack shrugged.

"She was weak," he declared, crossing his arms. "She couldn't handle life and fell apart. Last thing I heard, she was in California trying to get money for a drug-treatment center in Mexico."

Tyler moaned and dropped his head in his hands as the news of his beloved wife struck nearly unbearable sorrow in his heart. Elizabeth got a lump in her throat when she saw tears welling up in his eyes before he hid his face in his hands.

Jack's upper lip curled.

"Look, it's not my fault Rachel became an alcoholic," he said harshly. Tyler shook his head as he tried to close his mind against the burning in his chest at the sound of Rachel's name.

"She turned out to be a weak-minded, sniveling fool – which is why I divorced her and sent her packing," Jack continued, glancing at Tyler to see his reaction as he spoke.

Tyler slowly raised his head and fixed his blue eyes on Jack's dark eyes. The tears in his old partner's eyes didn't move Jack in the slightest.

"She called me a couple of months ago, wanting money," he said, as if simply recounting an uninteresting old story. "I told

21

her I wasn't going to throw good money away and to go get a job. For all I know, she could have been pregnant and just wanted enough to get an abortion. I don't know where she is...and I don't care."

Tyler's lips were trembling, but he didn't break his eye contact with Jack.

"You caused Tyler's children to abandon him with their mother," Elizabeth cried. "You robbed him of his livelihood – *and* his life's savings!"

"Your brother is weak, just like his wife!" Jack snarled, his eyes flashing. He finally looked away from Tyler as he rounded on Elizabeth. "It's not my fault she's a drug junkie and it's not my fault he didn't get the brakes on his car looked at before the accident."

"But you *knew* about the brakes, and you still didn't do a thing to help him!" Elizabeth shouted.

She took a few steps toward Jack, who stood with his arms folded, regarding her like he would a pesky fly.

"*Look* at all the damage you've caused!" she shouted in his face, trying to get some kind of response from him, but Jack merely stared at her, his eyes icy and hard as black marbles. Elizabeth, her hands shaking with fury and her heart bleeding for her brother, wanted nothing more than to strike his smirking face with all her might, but Tyler spoke up behind her.

"Lizzie, that's enough," he said firmly. "Let it go. All of these issues are in the past. It's time to move on."

Elizabeth took a deep, shuddering breath. She turned away from Jack to face her brother.

"But Tyler, it's not right!" she wailed, her voice now choked with unshed tears. "You treated him like a brother. You helped him build a profitable real-estate business. You made him rich. And all he ever did was swindle you, and hurt you and your family!"

Tyler reached for his sister's hand and held it tightly while she knelt beside the wheelchair, tightening her lips to keep from crying.

"Shh...I'm okay, Lizzie. We'll be fine, alright?" he whispered, patting her hand. She blinked hard, then stood up abruptly and walked over to the window, arms crossed with her back to the men.

Jack watched this scene with pitiless eyes. He even cracked a smile of amusement, looking from Tyler to Elizabeth, his arms still folded, as if he couldn't understand what would grieve Elizabeth so.

"Jack, what's going on?" Tyler asked him, forcing down the emotions roaring inside him. "We don't hear from you for over a year, then you suddenly show up on our doorstep. You're upsetting my sister, so what's this all about?"

Jack relaxed his arms and folded his hands behind his back.

"Tyler," he began, starting to pace a few steps back and forth in front of the wheelchair. "Do you remember when we bought this piece of property, how you and I both thought it had a lot of potential? We knew – even back then – that it could become one of the most lucrative land deals we ever made."

Tyler wrinkled his brow.

"Yes, I remember," he said, "This property does have immense potential. And one of these days," he added in a stronger voice, "when I get my health back, I plan to turn that potential into reality."

Jack threw back his head, his bruising laughter ringing out over the small room.

"Come on, Tyler," he gasped, trying to regain his breath from his own entertainment. "You and I both know that's never going to happen!" Then he suddenly grew serious.

"The truth is," he said, "I've already got the whole deal all wrapped up...and I didn't need your help to do it."

"What?" said Tyler, his eyes growing wide. "How is that possible?" Elizabeth turned around from facing the window.

GOOD & EVIL

"How can *you* have something in the works with *my* land?" Tyler asked.

Jack walked to within a few steps of Tyler's wheelchair and bent down so that his dark eyes were level with Tyler's blue ones.

"Tyler, I've got news for you," he said in a diplomatic voice. "This is *my* land now, not yours.

And I'm evicting you and your sorry sister."

Tyler sharply drew in his breath as the news hit him full force. Jack's cold eyes bored into Tyler's as the businessman watched the man in the wheelchair bowing under the burden Jack had suddenly thrust on his shoulders. Elizabeth put her hand over her mouth and gasped.

"But...but that can't be!" Tyler finally cried, staring up at Jack, his voice filled with despair.

"Ah, but it is, Tyler," Jack said coolly. He walked over to one of the old chairs opposite Tyler and sat down, folding his hands comfortably with both elbows propped up on the arms of the chair.

"Several years ago, when you were in my office signing some papers for another land deal, I slipped in an extra set of papers at the same time," Jack said to Tyler, who was staring at his lap as if he couldn't believe what he had just been told. "When you signed the extra set, you relinquished all *your* rights to this property...and signed them over to *me!*"

"I did no such thing!" Tyler cried, his voice shaking. "I never intended to–"

"It has nothing to do with intentions, Tyler, it has to do with reality!" Jack suddenly leaned forward, all his false posturing gone and his vicious, inexorable side rearing its head. He stood up.

"What a poor businessman you are," he spat at Tyler. "You've always been so trusting. You've always been an optimist. To you, the glass is always half full, never half empty."

"You've got that right," Tyler raised his head, his blue eyes now hard and bright. "I would much rather go through life trying to find the good in people, rather than the bad."

24

"Yes, that describes you perfectly," Jack sneered. "You've always been one to see only the 'good' in people instead of wisely seeing their many obvious faults."

"Yes, because I believe that's how every person ought to live," said Tyler with conviction. He looked over at his sister, who still stood by the window, listening. Elizabeth met his eyes, then looked down at the floor.

"Oh?" Jack replied, folding his arms. "You have lived by your 'Christian principles' this long – and look where it's brought you..."

Jack leaned down again in front of Tyler.

"You have *nothing*," he almost whispered, his voice full of unnerving satisfaction.

"I, I have this house," Tyler stammered. "And I have–"

"No, Tyler, you don't," Jack told him. He stood up and straightened his sports jacket. "In just a few short weeks, workers will be arriving with orders to level this place to the ground."

Elizabeth rushed forward, this time her face was lined with fear.

"No, Jack!" she pleaded. "You can't – "

Jack turned to face her, his gaze absolutely merciless.

"Oh, my dear Miss Emerson," he smiled. "But I can and I will. Your brother was never strong enough or tough enough to do it to them before they did it to him. And I must say, Tyler..." he added, glancing back at his old partner, "it was worth taking time off from work to tell you this in person, just so I could see the looks on your faces when I broke the news."

Tyler gazed up at the man in front of him who had taken apart his life piece by piece until he had finally destroyed it. Then he looked at his sister, whose face was as white as paper as she stared, open-mouthed, at Jack Krantz.

"You have no heart!" she said suddenly, her breath coming in quick gasps. "You have no feelings at all! You–"

25

"Lizzie," murmured Tyler, trying to calm his sister while trying to choke down the panic rising in his own chest. He swallowed hard and addressed his old friend.

"Jack..." Tyler searched for words. "Surely...you can't be serious."

Jack raised his fine, dark eyebrows.

"Oh, but I am," he stated. "I am *deadly* serious. The two of you have exactly two weeks to vacate these premises, so –"

"But–"

"...pack up and get out!" Jack finished relentlessly.

"You're crazy!" shouted Elizabeth. "This land is all Tyler has! You can't do this to us!"

Jack bowed with sinister politeness.

"I already *have* done it, Miss Emerson."

Jack looked at the brother and sister who were now looking at one another in hopeless despair. He started to laugh again.

"Look at the two of you! Both of you are complete idiots. You're nothing but do-gooders who don't have enough sense to look out for your own best interests. Look at the benefits your precious 'Christianity' has brought you now! Tyler, you are nothing but a cripple with no income..."

Jack ticked the losses off on his fingers as he listed them.

"...You've got no friends. And now, you have nowhere to live."

Tyler shook his head, disbelief still screaming in his mind. "You can't mean you're just kicking us out?"

Jack sneered. "Just like that. I want you off my property, Tyler Emerson. You have exactly thirty days. Not one hour more."

Jack looked at the small room around him.

"I'm going to bulldoze this miserable shack to the ground," he said, glancing at Elizabeth out of the corner of his eye.

She was staring at him with so much hatred in her eyes that Jack felt an irresistible urge to goad her on.

"You see?" he said to her, spreading his hands, "No matter how much you yell at me, you can't beat me. I win. I will always

26

win. And *you*–" He turned and pointed at Tyler, "will always lose."

Jack walked back over to the broken man in the wheelchair. Elizabeth had knelt down beside her brother with her hand on his shoulder. Her eyes were clouded with fear.

Jack reached into a pocket inside his sports jacket and pulled out the envelope Judith had given him earlier. Jack held it up, then let it drop onto Tyler's lap.

"Here's your legal eviction notice," he said. Then he leaned down so he could look into Tyler's bewildered eyes one last time.

"It was good to see you again, *old friend*," Jack said softly with a poisonous smirk. He gave Tyler a smart slap on the knee and walked away with a triumphant smile, leaving the pair of shattered lives behind him.

As the screen door slammed behind Jack, Tyler bowed his head over his lap, breathing hard. With shaking hands he fingered the eviction papers on his knee. Had it really come to this? Was Jack right? Tyler had spent his whole life faithfully trusting God to carry him through the rough times as well as the good, and now he truly had lost everything...

No, Tyler abruptly thought to himself.

He turned to his sister, whose eyes were filled with tears.

"Hey, hey," he said gently, taking both her hands in his. "We're going to be just fine, you hear me? Don't be afraid. God will take care of us."

"But how, Tyler? What are we going to do? I've been with you ever since Rachel left and you at least had a place to call your own–"

"Hey," Tyler cut in, "You've taken good care of me, Lizzie. I couldn't ask for a better sister. And we'll figure something out. God will help us."

Elizabeth's face hardened. "You keep saying that, but I don't see how God is going to be able to get us out of this mess... unless He decides to just miraculously drop a new house in front of us."

"Lizzie, don't lose your trust in God," said Tyler firmly. "It could be worse."

"Worse?" cried his sister, jumping up. *"Worse?* How can you, of all people, say that? Tyler, you've been hurt. You've been mistreated. You've lost so much. You've suffered in ways nobody should have to, and yet you still act like everything's okay."

"God loves us, Lizzie," Tyler said quietly, looking into her eyes. "He isn't the cause of all this. We need to trust in Him now more than ever."

Elizabeth just looked at him, her eyes clouding over with tears. Then she turned away and ran from the room. Slamming the door to her bedroom behind her, Elizabeth flung herself across her bed and began to sob as she succumbed to the hopelessness and despair flooding through her.

Tyler sat alone in the empty, shabby living room in his wheelchair, listening helplessly to the faint sound of his sister's sobs. Struggling against the grief, anger and fear threatening to overwhelm him, Tyler put his head in his hands again, this time in fervent prayer that God would forgive him for the anger in his heart over Jack's cutting words. The Emersons were desperate. They had no money and nowhere to go. And now they had no more time.

"He who sins is of the devil, for the devil has sinned from the beginning. For this purpose the Son of God was manifested, that He might destroy the works of the devil."
-1 John 3:8

CHAPTER 4: THE ACCIDENT

With a smile on his face, Jack Krantz stepped out onto the front porch and looked around at what now all belonged to him. It felt good to finally be rid of his old partner and win again. He plucked his sunglasses out and began putting them on as he headed toward his car.

Jack took a quick step down onto the top porch step, unaware that the rickety, old, termite-ridden planks could no longer hold his weight. Jack's foot broke through the weathered, wooden step and he felt himself flying forward with nothing to stop his fall. He waved his arms wildly and his body twisted in a desperate effort to catch hold of the porch railing, but instead his flailing hand knocked over the garden rake Elizabeth had set there earlier. The rake flipped over the railing and toppled down, landing on the grass with its four sharp prongs pointing straight upward. Jack, unable to catch his balance, let out a cry as he landed with a thud on his back. He fell right on top of the upturned rake, and the sharp prongs sunk into his back all the way down to their metal base, piercing into his chest cavity.

Jack lay helplessly on the ground, common sense warning him not to move as he stared up at the leafy branches of the majestic old oak tree. In his shock, he was aware that something was seriously wrong. Every small rise and fall of his chest when he breathed caused a burning pain to radiate through his torso. He felt something by his outstretched arm, and turning his head ever so slightly to the left, saw his dark sunglasses lying near him. As he looked at them, they grew more and more hazy. Gazing back up at the tree and seeing sunlight between the leaves, Jack's eyes blinked to a close as he slipped into unconsciousness...

Tyler raised his head at the sound of wood cracking and something hitting the ground outside. Curious, he called his sister but she did not reply. He began wheeling himself toward the front door, again calling to Elizabeth. She appeared in the doorway to the living room.

29

"What is it, Tyler?"

"I thought I heard something outside," he explained.

"Okay," she sighed, opening the screen door. "I'll go check it out."

Elizabeth opened the front door and took two steps out onto the front porch and stopped cold. She didn't make a sound. Tyler sat up, waiting for her to tell him what happened. He saw her through the screen door standing on the porch, staring out into the yard.

"Lizzie?" he called impatiently. "What is it?"

Elizabeth seemed to shake herself out of her trance, and suddenly to his surprise she let out a short laugh of astonishment mingled with ridicule.

"Tyler!" she said with a snicker, "it's Jack. He fell down the steps."

Tyler wheeled himself up to the front door. Elizabeth turned and opened the screen door to help Tyler make his way out the door onto the porch. Elizabeth walked down the ramp over to where Jack Krantz lay motionless on the ground. As Elizabeth looked down at him, she was surprised to see he wasn't getting up and that his eyes were closed. Now faintly alarmed, she knelt down beside the wounded man and saw the blood seeping through his shirt.

"Tyler, this is serious. Jack's unconscious," she called back to her brother on the porch. "He's bleeding..."

Elizabeth's voice trailed off as she gingerly lifted the man's wrist and felt for his pulse.

"Is he breathing?" Tyler called, concerned.

Elizabeth tilted her face down towards Jack's head with her ear near his slightly parted lips. She grimaced when she felt his faint, warm breath on her cheek. This was closer to Jack Krantz than she ever wanted to be.

"Yes, he's breathing," she told her brother, sitting back on her heels. "And I can feel a pulse but it doesn't seem to be very strong. He looks pretty bad, Tyler. I think he's in shock."

"Where is the bleeding coming from?"

Elizabeth shrugged. "I don't know..."

Then she saw the long handle of the garden rake protruding from underneath the fallen man.

"It looks like Jack somehow knocked over the garden rake and fell on it!" For the second time she grimaced, but this time with horror. Just the thought of having those rake prongs sunk inside someone, even if that person was her worst enemy, made cold shivers run up and down her spine. She swallowed hard.

"What?"

"The rake...he fell on the rake."

As Elizabeth turned back to speak to her brother, she spied the broken porch step.

Getting to her feet and examining the rotted wood, she began to realize what had happened "That old step must have given way under Jack's weight, then my guess is he hit the rake as he fell and landed on it," she said in a matter-of-fact tone.

Tyler's face grew pale.

"Lizzie," he called with great concern, "quick, call 911. We've got to get Jack some help immediately."

To Tyler's surprise, Elizabeth didn't move.

"Lizzie, come on!" he cried, wondering why she just stood there. He knew she had the cell phone with her, their only connection to the outside world. "You need to call for help. Right now!"

But Elizabeth bit her lip and stayed where she was. She turned and looked back at Jack, then at her brother. Even from the porch Tyler could see the defiance in her face.

"Did you hear me, Lizzie? Don't waste time! Jack needs our help now!"

"Tyler, I'm not convinced we *should* help Jack," Elizabeth said firmly. "He came here today to ruin us. He admitted that he cheated you out of your land. He's planning to evict us and leave us with nothing. And you *know*," she added, raising her voice, "the other horrible things he's done to you! Why should we help him?"

Tyler stared at his sister. "Lizzie, do you hear what you are saying?" he cried in horror. "Have you lost your mind? We can't just stand by idly and do nothing while Jack lies there and bleeds to death. He needs help. Please call for help. *Now!*"

Tyler's anxiety turned to irritation when his sister slowly turned her head to the side and remained standing firmly in place.

"Well then, at least give me the phone so *I* can call!" he demanded, his voice heated now. Tyler wheeled closer to the steps and in desperation outstretched his arm toward Elizabeth.

"Tyler, do you think if it were you or me lying there that Jack would lift so much as a finger to help us?" Elizabeth argued coldly, waving her hand to indicate the unconscious man. "Not a chance! He would step over us and never look back once. I say we treat him exactly like he's treated you. I say..." Elizabeth paused, then turned to look back at her brother.

"I say, let the rotten jerk die," she said harshly.

"No, Lizzie, no!" Tyler cried in dismay. "I can't believe I'm hearing this from you! You know better than that. We never help ourselves by hurting someone else. No matter what Jack has done we must do what is right. We are to treat others the way we want to be treated."

Elizabeth rolled her eyes and exhaled sharply.

"Don't start quoting Bible stuff to me, Tyler," she warned him. "I don't want to hear–"

"Lizzie, we've been raised to always do the right thing in God's sight," Tyler told her earnestly, leaning forward in his wheelchair. "And I'm not about to stop now," he added firmly. "I will not be a party to murder – which is exactly what this will be if we don't help Jack! Now please, call 911...if not for Jack then do it for my sake!"

Elizabeth finally conceded, but her heart was filled with reluctance as she slowly pulled a battered silver cell phone out of her pocket. Giving Tyler her most unenthusiastic expression, she dialed the number and began telling the operator what had happened. Finished with the call, she handed the phone to Tyler, telling him they were on the way, and then she turned and walked back into the house, wanting no more to do with helping Jack Krantz.

Tyler remained on the front porch. For a few seconds more he gazed over at his ex-partner lying on the ground. He then bowed his head and began to pray.

Out in the yard, the outstretched body of Jack Krantz remained motionless.

"...Michael the archangel, in contending with the devil, when he disputed about the body of Moses, dared not bring against him a reviling accusation, but said, 'The Lord rebuke you!'"   **-Jude 1:9**

The yard was silent. Not a breath of wind stirred the leaves of the tall oak tree. The injured man laid alone, his life slowly bleeding away. Tyler Emerson still sat in his wheelchair on the porch, praying. From time to time he looked over at Jack to see if anything about the wounded man had changed. Then he looked down the road, listening intently for the sound of ambulance sirens.

Then, there was a stirring in the air as the wind suddenly picked up and swirled around like a small whirlwind, moving across the yard toward where Jack lay. The whirlwind seem to collapse and something appeared in the yard as if born from the gust of wind.

A being in the likeness of a man, dressed from head to foot in black, walked slowly over to Jack. The figure moved fluidly, his jet-black hair unaffected by the breeze, as though time had no effect or power over him at all. He finally came to a standstill by Jack, standing over him with a pair of shiny black shoes planted on the ground near Jack's head. This being stood silently for a moment, studying the man on the ground with the rake prongs in his back as intently as a lion watches the prey it is about to seize. Then the being's wicked face cracked into a malevolent smile.

"Oh yes, yes," he whispered in a rough, dark voice that seemed to come from a heavy fog. "Long have I waited for this day. Jack Krantz, your entire life you have been the poster boy for every kind of evil imaginable–hatred, corruption, deception, thievery, and a thousand more vices just like them. You, my friend," the being addressed the unconscious man, "are quite a catch."

The black-garbed figure's eyes glowed maliciously. As his eyes lit up the pupils burned a distinct blood-red while he gazed down on Jack. An aura of menace surrounded his presence.

Suddenly the wind picked up again and began to swirl. The dark spirit turned toward it, his satisfied smile slipping to an annoyed and surprised frown. Another being, similar to the first in

35

bearing semblance to a man, appeared. Unlike the dark spirit being whose skin resembled the flesh of a cadaver, the light spirit had a skin tone of soft olive, and he had white hair whereas the dark spirit's hair was coal black. The second being was dressed all in white, and radiated a soft ethereal glow. When the dark spirit saw the light spirit, he growled and took a step closer to Jack as though staking a claim over him.

"What are *you* doing here?" he demanded in a mocking voice. "I never cease to be amazed. You show up when there's absolutely no chance of your side winning this battle. Jack Krantz is *mine*. So, until the appointed time, go busy yourself elsewhere."

The evil spirit moved around Jack so he was positioned between the man and the good spirit. His lips curled back from his teeth in a snarl like a ravenous wolf that has been interrupted during a meal.

Unperturbed, the good spirit moved lightly towards the evil spirit, a quiet smile on his face. He, too, seemed to drift through the air without time's pressure bearing on him. As he approached, the evil spirit bared his teeth at him again and took a possessive step back closer to Jack. Soon the two spirits were both at a standstill with Jack between them. The good spirit disregarded the black scowls of the dark spirit as he studied Jack.

"It sounds like someone is overconfident," he said calmly. His voice was soft and soothing as if it came out of a dream. He looked down at the wounded man with beautiful sky-blue eyes... eyes with pure white pupils that slowly glowed brighter and brighter as he studied Jack.

"He isn't dead yet, and you have already consigned him to hell," the good spirit said to the evil spirit, gesturing toward Jack. "Give the guy a chance. He might surprise you." And here the good spirit chuckled. "Why, I might be the one taking him, while you end up empty-handed."

The evil spirit shook his head. "Not a chance of *that* happening! You obviously don't know this man at all, whereas I, on the other hand, know him *very* well."

The evil spirit spread his hands out over the injured man between them.

"He's a complete charlatan," the evil spirit said. "He's a liar, a thief, and an adulterer. In fact, he's just plain evil – through and through. And I'm proud to say I've helped him time and again to learn that."

The evil spirit rubbed his hands together and smiled delightedly as he spoke of Jack Krantz's blackened life. But the good spirit shook his head.

"Maybe he is evil," he said, looking sadly down at Jack. "But as you and I both know, humans aren't *born* that way. They start out clean and pure, and then, on occasion, along the way some of them turn into the Jack Krantzes of this world."

"Ha! What do you mean, 'some' of them?" said the evil spirit. "Most *all* of them are like Jack Krantz in one way or another."

"Perhaps," said the good spirit. "But it doesn't *have* to be that way. And until they draw their final breath, nothing is locked in stone. People can change, you know."

Their conversation was interrupted by the arrival of an ambulance. As the paramedics jumped out of the ambulance and rushed over to Jack, the two spirits moved away from the wounded man to watch the EMTs stabilize the injured man.

"Is he going to be okay?" Tyler called anxiously from the porch as the paramedics began working over Jack.

"Give us a minute, sir," one of them responded.

When they carefully turned Jack over, there was the rake with the metal forks buried deep in his back. Tyler flinched.

The paramedics secured two belts around Jack to keep the rake and its handle from moving and causing him more harm before they lifted him onto the gurney. They couldn't take the rake out of him there, for to pry it from the wound would mean Jack's bleeding to death. The rake would have to be removed from his body at the hospital.

GOOD & EVIL

All this time, no one saw the spirit of light and the spirit of darkness standing off to the side, watching closely.

"You know, *my* king began his work in the Garden of Eden with a lie that caused the first humans to sin," the evil spirit said proudly. He was leaning against the big tree with casual ease. The good spirit stood several feet away from him, his blue eyes with the white pupils glowing.

"*My* king used the lust of the flesh, the lust of the eye and the pride of life," the evil spirit went on boastfully. "These have worked well for us from that first sin on earth."

"Your king may in fact be the king of the earth," the good spirit acknowledged, "but God did not create the earth for Satan. God created the world for His Son Jesus, and all that was made was made through Him."

The good spirit spoke of Satan as if his tongue shied away from the name. At his statement, the evil spirit glowered at him.

Elizabeth had come out of the house when she heard the ambulance arrive. She joined Tyler on the front porch to see what the paramedics would say about Jack's condition, wondering if maybe he was dead. The Emersons watched as their enemy, the man who had ruined their lives, was being treated. Elizabeth, her face devoid of pity, stood with one arm wrapped around one of the porch posts, leaning against the porch railing as she observed the scene. Behind her Tyler sat in his wheelchair but, instead of looking at Jack, his eyes were closed, his head was bowed and he was moving his lips in more silent prayer.

Unseen by both brother and sister, the two spirits stood on the porch with them as they also watched Jack Krantz being loaded onto a gurney and lifted into the ambulance.

"So you think the likes of Jack Krantz can *change?*" demanded the evil spirit of the good spirit. "You really live in a dream world all your own, don't you?"

The good spirit laughed softly. "Oh, it's no dream. Humans aren't as untrustworthy as you make them out to be."

"Yeah right!" the evil spirit said rudely. "Leave the ivory

38

halls of your sanctified realm for a while and then you'll see what this is all about. Humans may start out with a clean slate but they rarely end up with one. Admit it: more often than not, what they do best is *sin*."

"I disagree," the good spirit replied. "Sure, humans make mistakes along the way. But there are two things you have overlooked."

The evil spirit scoffed. "Oh yes? What did I overlook?"

"First," the good spirit began, "they have lots of help. You and your cohorts tempt and entice them at every turn, do you not?"

The evil spirit smiled wickedly. "Of course we do. We've been lying to the humans from the beginning. We're not ashamed to admit it. We've got just one goal. We want everyone in our corner and no one in yours. It's that simple."

"And that's your entire agenda – eternal destruction of the whole human race," said the good spirit.

"Sure. It's that simple," the evil spirit repeated proudly. "Most human beings don't believe there is a hell, but you and I know there is. Maybe it helps them sleep better at night to deny its existence. And if you get them to think there really are no eternal consequences, they'll have no trouble sinning. That's our agenda. It's no secret. And you can't deny that we're successful!" he added with a jeer.

The good spirit looked over at the man being put into the ambulance. Then he turned to study the man in the wheelchair. Then he looked back at the evil spirit, whose face was gloating.

"And exactly how do you measure your 'success'?" he inquired.

The evil spirit grinned.

"Look at the numbers. We have way more people than you do. There's no comparison. We win. You lose," he declared with wicked finality.

"Why the arrogant attitude?" questioned the good spirit mildly. "How can you be so sure? How do you know you have this 'all locked up'?"

"Listen to yourself! Jesus Himself said: 'Wide is the gate and broad is the way that leads to destruction, and there are many who go in by it.'" The evil spirit sneered as he spat the words out of his mouth as if he tasted something foul. "We are virtually guaranteed to win!"

The good spirit, glowing full of light, shook his head again. His bright eyes danced.

"That isn't entirely true," he stated, and the evil spirit glared at him. "You *don't* win. God knows not every soul will be saved. He knew that from the beginning, so you haven't beaten Him. Just because you end up with more souls doesn't mean you win."

"We almost got all of them at the time of the Flood, remember?" the evil spirit interrupted.

"And yet, eight souls were saved, remember?" the good spirit said, smiling at the frustration his reply sparked in the evil spirit's red eyes.

You can't really claim success until you achieve your ultimate goal—the destruction of *all* mankind," the good spirit added.

"Well, we're well on our way to that, aren't we!" said the evil spirit, standing with his back against the wall and one foot propped up behind him, arms folded. He seemed utterly confident in his statement.

"How so?" the good spirit asked. He was leaning against the porch railing near Elizabeth, who hadn't moved from her position.

The evil spirit straightened up, an evil, eager fire in his red eyes.

"We use every dirty trick in the book. We use deception to make it appear that we're telling the truth, when in fact we're not. We convince humans they're right when really, they're wrong. These humans are so gullible. They believe a lie faster than they will believe God and we count on that."

"Not all humans are as gullible as you think," said the good spirit quietly but defensively.

"Ha, they accept so easily a little lie mixed with the truth!" cried the evil spirit. "That's one of our best methods for getting religious humans to believe a lie – stir a little truth into it. Then they are so willing to teach that lie to others..."

"And so, the lethal infection grows," said the good spirit, his voice calm but with a dark edge to it.

"Precisely." The evil spirit grinned. "And we have a list of lies that are notorious for getting the religiously minded humans to disobey God."

"I know you do," said the good spirit, his face displeased. He folded his arms, which goaded the evil spirit on.

"The one I like best is, 'if you were ever saved, you will always be saved.' That's a great one," he said with a laugh as he thought over his past triumphs using that lie. "Or the feel-good deception that 'everyone is going to Heaven.'"

The evil spirit wrinkled his brow as he thought through his arsenal of corruption. "One of my favorite church lies is that you can worship at the church of your choice. And then there's the lie, 'I have done more good than bad'."

The evil spirit continued naming off the lies in his inventory.

"And this one, 'Take Jesus into your heart and you will be saved'. That one works remarkably well," the dark spirit gloated.

"Because they have to do more than that to be accepted by God," the good spirit said.

"Yes, but when I can get them to believe that's all they have to do, accept Jesus into their heart and that's all, then I've got them," the evil spirit grinned. "And here's my favorite: 'It's okay to worship other gods and follow men instead of Jesus'. Need I go on?"

"You are right. Those lies will cause many to lose their souls," the good spirit said with a sigh.

The evil spirit leaned back against the wall of the house, grinning triumphantly at his nemesis.

"But surely you are aware how easily truth can prevail over these lies if humans only seek after it?" the good spirit added quickly, and the evil spirit's smirk slipped just the slightest bit.

Out in the yard, the paramedics had finished loading Jack Krantz into the ambulance. Under the eyes of Tyler and Elizabeth the medical vehicle drove away, transporting Jack to the hospital. The scream of the ambulance siren slowly melted away into the warm afternoon, leaving the old house and property quiet once again. For now, the Emersons would be safe from their persecutor.

Elizabeth stood with folded arms as the ambulance left. Her eyes narrowed to sharp slits after it.

"Let's hope he's DOA," she muttered, turning to go back into the house.

Tyler jerked his head up.

"Elizabeth Rose Emerson, how can you wish for such a thing? God says we are to pray for our enemies and do good to those who spitefully use us. I know Jack has wronged us terribly, but we have no right to wish evil upon him."

His sister's face twisted in an unmistakable scowl, and Tyler knew how angry she was.

"No, Tyler." She held her hand up. "Don't you start quoting the Bible to me again. I can't take it right now."

She stormed into the house, slamming the screen door behind her.

Brokenhearted and disappointed, with tears in his eyes, Tyler began once more to pray – not only for Jack's healing, but for the anger in his own sister's heart.

In the distance the loud cry of the ambulance siren was fading away.

"We know that we are of God, and the whole world lies under the sway of the wicked one."　　　　　　　　　　　　　　　　　　　*-1 John 5:19*

With lights flashing and the siren wailing, the ambulance bearing Jack Krantz turned out of the lane onto the main highway and headed toward the nearest hospital. The driver called ahead to inform the hospital staff that they were on their way with an emergency patient in critical condition.

In the back of the ambulance, the other paramedics continued to monitor Jack's IV and vital signs, and started him on oxygen. The two spirits sat one on either side of the gurney on which Jack lay, unseen and unheard by the humans.

"You're still missing the big picture," said the good spirit earnestly. "You didn't quote the entire passage when you referred to the Scriptures earlier."

"As if it matters?" scoffed the evil spirit. He had one hand placed on the side of the gurney, as if still laying claim to the man on it.

"It *does* matter. Jesus went on to say that 'narrow is the gate and difficult is the way which leads to life, and there are few who find it'. It doesn't say that *none* will find the way; it says that *few* will!"

"So what's your point?" the evil spirit demanded. "For all practical purposes, *we* are still in the majority. In the end *we* still win."

"Being in the majority is not the same as winning," said the good spirit patiently. Now he also had his hand on the gurney. "Truth is not determined by majority opinion or popular vote. You and I both know that..."

The evil spirit hissed, his red eyes glowing balefully.

"We both know", the good spirit said confidently, "you are *never* going to win. It's just not going to happen."

"What are you talking about?" the evil spirit snarled. Then his eyes widened in comprehension. "Wait a minute. Does this have something to do with what you said earlier when you told me there were *two* things I overlooked?"

GOOD & EVIL

"Yes it does. Face it: more often than you would like to admit it, humans surprise you," said the good spirit with a smile.

"How so?"

"By intentionally abandoning evil and choosing to do good. If Jack Krantz is the model for evil, then Tyler Emerson is the model for good. He, and others like him, shatter the lie to your claim that evil triumphs. It never has and it never will."

The evil spirit laughed. "HA! Evil has the clear advantage! And your own Scriptures state as much. God said that 'the heart is deceitful above all things, and is desperately wicked'?"

"Ah, but once again you have overlooked the important point of how humans were created," said the good spirit patiently.

"What's that got to do with it?"

"Much. Certainly, God gave them free will. And yes, they can use that free will to choose to sin," said the good spirit.

"And they do – *a lot*," said the evil spirit smugly. "The Bible says all people have sinned and fallen short of God's expectations."

"But they can also use that free will to correct their mistakes," the good spirit explained. "You said that Jack Krantz is an adulterer. So was King David. But was it not the same King David who said after repenting of his sin: 'O God, create in me a clean heart, and renew a steadfast spirit within me'?"

"What's your point?"

"My point is this. Here you are, hovering over Jack Krantz, waiting for him to breathe his last breath because you are certain you have him permanently under your spell."

"I've had him under my spell nearly his entire life!" the evil spirit declared with a triumphant grin.

"But what if he pulls a King David on you?" demanded the good spirit. His gentle face bore an expression of hard intensity as he looked at the evil spirit. "What if he survives, realizes the error of his ways, repents, and begs God: 'Create in me a clean heart, and renew a steadfast spirit within me.'?" The good spirit smiled. "People repent more than you would like to admit."

44

Thc ambulance reached the local hospital. Pulling into the emergency entrance, it backed up to the emergency room doors. Having stopped, the driver jumped out, ran around to the back and opened the doors of the ambulance, helping the other paramedics to bring Jack's gurney out of the medical vehicle. As they wheeled the gurney hurriedly in through the big doors that opened automatically to the emergency department, a doctor and two nurses rushed up to the gurney and took over the care of Jack from the EMTs, and Jack was taken to the trauma emergency area. As the trauma team ascertained Jack's situation, the room entered into a flurried state of organized chaos. Doctors and nurses gave brisk commands and orders for drugs and testing, only to conclude that Jack Krantz was in a very critical condition and would need immediate emergency surgery to extricate the rake from his body. Hopefully, through heart surgery, they would be able to save his life.

As the doctors and nurses busied themselves in a flurry of urgent activity around Jack, once again nobody was aware of the two spirits in the room who were observing the patient's treatment. One sat on a cabinet in the far corner of the room, eying Jack the way a hunched black vulture looks down on its prey. The other spirit sat on the empty examination table beside the one Jack was on, his blue eyes with the bright white pupils glowing thoughtfully. For a while neither of the spirits spoke to each other as they watched the trauma team working fiercely to keep Jack alive.

"So you think Krantz is going to be revived and somehow walk out of here a 'changed man'?" the evil spirit said skeptically. "I doubt it."

"As I said, it has happened before," the good spirit replied. "In fact, stranger things have happened. You remember the story of King Manasseh of Judah, do you not?"

The evil spirit rolled his eyes and sighed in exasperation. "What has an ancient king got to do with Jack Krantz?"

"The Bible says that the king 'misled Judah so that the people did more evil than the nations whom the Lord has destroyed

45

before the people of Israel. Manasseh shed much innocent blood, until he had filled Jerusalem from one end to the other.'"

"Sounds like my kind of guy!" the evil spirit said happily.

"Not so fast!" the good spirit warned. "Listen to the rest of the story. It turns out that Manasseh was defeated by the king of Assyria and was carried away in shackles as a slave."

"And this helps you *how*?" the evil spirit wondered.

"The story doesn't end there either," the good spirit went on. "Manasseh repented and prayed to God for forgiveness."

The evil spirit shuddered.

"Is this going to be another one of those 'King David' type of bedtime stories?"

"The Bible said that 'God received his entreaty, heard his plea, and restored him again to Jerusalem and to his kingdom. Then Manasseh knew that the Lord indeed was God.' The same kind of thing *could* happen to Jack Krantz," the good spirit said fervently.

The two spirits looked back over at the examination table. A copious amount of blood was visible, and the doctors were working frantically over Jack. One of the doctors, Doctor Daniels, came over with an X-ray photograph in his hand to speak to one of the trauma team members in charge.

"One of those rake prongs clipped his heart," Doctor Daniels said urgently, holding up the X-ray. The picture of Jack's chest cavity clearly indicated the sharp prongs sunk deep in his body, and one of the rusty points had entered his right ventricle.

"Get Dr. Kelly! This man needs surgery now!"

The rush of activity now moved faster than ever.

The evil spirit turned back to the spirit in white, who stood with arms folded, a small smile of optimism on his face.

"I keep telling you, this guy is *mine*," the evil spirit bragged. "You know what he's like. He stole his partner's wife, cheated him out of his future, and evicted him from his home. Not to mention everything else he's ever done that violates honor and truth. The word 'repent' isn't even in Krantz's vocabulary!"

"Are you sure about that?" the good spirit questioned. "That's what people thought about another king of Judah – Jehoshaphat."

"Oh boy, you've got a thousand of these king stories, don't you?"

"You would do well to listen," answered the good spirit, his bright eyes flashing. "There is an important moral here. Jehoshaphat started out as a good king but then made an evil alliance with the wicked king of Israel, Ahab. Jehu the prophet said to Jehoshaphat, 'Should you help the wicked and love those who hate the Lord? Because of this, wrath has gone out against you from the Lord.'"

"Once again," the evil spirit spread his hands in a mockingly curious manner. "I ask you: how does this help your case?"

"The Bible goes on to state that the king repented of his evil actions and 'went out again among the people...to bring them back to the God of their ancestors.'" the good spirit said. "Don't give up on people so quickly – even the likes of Jack Krantz."

"Look," said the evil spirit harshly, "David, Manasseh and Jehoshaphat *started out* good. Jack Krantz doesn't have a good bone in his body. He's been bad all his life."

The good spirit smiled quietly. "Are you sure about that?"

"Absolutely!" cried the evil spirit. "The guy is evil – through and through. He's got no interest in repenting. He's self-centered, greedy and just plain *mean*. He loves to lie, steal, cheat... he'll *never* change."

"Ah, but he *could* change, given the right incentive and information," the good spirit declared. "You know the old saying, 'there are no atheists in foxholes.' Well, there aren't any atheists on hospital gurneys either. Jack Krantz has certainly been provided with the incentive to cause him to repent!"

"Big deal! Suppose he doesn't survive the rake poking into his heart? Suppose he dies on the operating table? *Then* I've got him!"

"True," said the good spirit simply. "But what if he *does* survive? Suppose he makes it through this ordeal. Then – whether you want to admit it or not – he *does* have a chance to repent, change his ways, and alter where he spends eternity."

"And I suppose you're going to tell me that if he survives there's someone out there just waiting to get the proper information to him about exactly what he would need to do to change his ways and get on the road to eternal glory?" the evil spirit said in a bored voice.

"You took the words right out of my mouth," the good spirit smiled. "God has always provided all the information people need to change their lives for the better."

"That hasn't helped Jack Krantz very much, has it?"

"But it could, because God has also guaranteed people *access* to that information. The psalmist–"

The evil spirit let out a long, heaving sigh. But the good spirit went on, undeterred.

"–Speaking on God's behalf, said: 'I love those who love Me, and those who seek Me diligently will *find Me*'. You would really hate for *that* to happen, wouldn't you – Jack Krantz 'finding' God?"

"That's never going to happen!" the evil spirit viciously shook his head. "Trust me. I know this man. He's rotten – side to side and top to bottom. There's not going to be any saving him. I've got him and you don't. You never will. Give up."

The dark spirit's red eyes narrowed as he looked into the white, glowing pupils of the good spirit. "Admit defeat." he hissed.

Just then, the doctors began rolling Jack's gurney out of the emergency room to take him to the operating room. The attending doctor turned to the nurse and said quietly, "He's lost a lot of blood, and I don't think either of the chambers on the right side of his heart are working at all. I don't think he's going to make it through the night."

Hearing this, the evil spirit smiled widely in a way that made him look even more dreadful than when he was glowering.

"You might as well go on," he told the good spirit, who folded his arms and cocked his head. "He'll be mine tonight."

The good spirit just smiled, but his blue eyes hardened determinedly.

"As humans say, 'I have all the time in the world'," he replied coolly. "And I think Jack still has a chance."

In the operating room the two spirits stood on either side of the operating table, looking over the shoulders of the surgeons from time to time to observe the surgical procedure to save Jack's life. Once again, neither spirit was seen or heard by the doctors swiftly working on Jack's heart.

The evil spirit's red eyes burned fiery hot as he became more and more excited about Jack's condition. In contrast, the good spirit stood with his hands behind his back, face calm, eyes bright with anticipation and a secretive smile on his face that greatly annoyed the dark spirit.

"It's so easy to get these humans to sin and lead them to hell," he at last remarked boastfully in an attempt to irritate the good spirit. The good spirit turned his head from looking at Jack to stare calmly at the evil spirit across the table.

"All we have to do is simply get them to disobey God by tempting them with their own petty desires. When that desire overrides their wanting to please God, we've got them," the evil spirit continued. "God Himself has condemned all to hell who don't follow the commandments of His Son Jesus. Only those pitiful few who actually do that will you be able to take to Heaven. Jack Krantz here was one of the easier targets."

He laughed recklessly.

"Why, I can get even the best of them to sin sometimes," he boasted.

"That may be true," said the good spirit softly. "But God gave His son Jesus to die a cruel and torturous death on the cross of Calvary to become the living sacrifice for *all* the sins of *all* mankind. And God the Father said by that sacrifice He would forgive any and *every one* of their sins *if* they were to become a faithful Christian and would confess their sin to God and truly repent of that sin in their life."

"But *we* teach them to think they are safe and righteous in God's sight when they're not!" the evil spirit declared triumphantly. "It's so easy to do! We have a great slogan: 'Worship at the church of *your* choice'. By using that, we get the miserable humans to believe they can worship God anywhere, any place, any time, any way they want. One of our best lies."

The good spirit looked as if he was about to speak, but the evil spirit wasn't finished.

"They simply don't pay attention to the fact that God has always been very strict about how and what He will accept as true worship to Him," he said smugly.

The good spirit's eyes saddened, but his gentle voice was firm.

"Again, there is a point there. Most humans are in fact involved in empty, vain worship God has not asked for. *But* Jesus has made it very clear what true worship is, and all have been given an opportunity to know and practice what *is* acceptable to God," he added with confidence.

"But my lies will get them to disobey God and then we have them," said the evil spirit gleefully. "It's so easy to lead them to hell. I just have to get the best of them to disregard the will of God. There are always the good old standbys like adultery, fornication, abortion, murder, stealing, lying, and all the sexual sins God hates."

"God has given all humans, through His Son Jesus, all they need to know to be saved from you and hell," said the good spirit firmly. "But He also gives them the choice to seek that information and act on it to be the godly people He will accept. That list of lies you brought up earlier may be extensive, but you can't force the humans to believe those lies. That's up to them, the same way it's up to them to choose for themselves whom they will serve: Jesus or Satan."

"Well, what about those atheistic lies we feed them?" the evil spirit went on, as though determined to prove to the good spirit how much he enjoyed what he did. "You know, there are many humans who fall for the lie that God doesn't even exist. When they believe that, it makes our job so much easier. We can get them to believe things like...there is no life after death, and God and Jesus don't exist."

The evil spirit burst into laughter. "Haha, I love to see their faces when they die and find out they were wrong!"

"I'm sure you enjoy it," said the good spirit dryly. His voice was flat.

"Oh, and here's a great one: the lie that God didn't create the earth, and make up all kinds of ridiculous ways God's creation got here."

"But you and I both know that God *did* create the earth some thousands of years ago," the good spirit reminded him. The evil spirit shrugged.

"But our lies keep them from believing that, and that also makes them say God lied. Nowadays with over 360,000 new humans entering the world each day, we have our work cut out for us in getting these condemned to hell–"

"Which is everlasting punishment for *all of you*," the good spirit interrupted. For the first time since he had appeared in the Emersons' yard, his soft eyes began burning an intensely white-hot.

"You know that in the end you will be subject to eternal punishment as much as those who reject God," he told the evil spirit. "Hell is not reserved for human beings alone."

"Therefore submit to God. Resist the devil and he will flee from you."
-James 4:7

The doctors finished the extensive surgery on Jack and moved him to a room in the Intensive Care Unit where he would spend the next several days recovering from the open-heart surgery he had undergone. The doctors kept him heavily sedated, morphine trickling through his system by way of an IV and plastic oxygen tubes attached, and he was kept connected to machines that monitored his heart, blood pressure, and respiratory rate. Bright light from florescent bulbs filled the room. A nurse was recording Jack's vital signs on a computer when Dr. Richard Kelly, the young surgeon who had overseen Jack's surgery, entered the room and began reading the information the nurse had already recorded. He also inspected the surgical wound area for anything unusual.

As Dr. Kelly checked the monitor that indicated Jack's vital signs, he began speaking almost as if he was thinking out loud.

"This fellow sure is lucky to be alive," he remarked, shaking his head as he looked down at the unconscious patient. "He had a tough surgery."

Dr. Kelly turned around to address the nurse.

"We had to restart his heart three times during the operation," he said, a note of incredulity in his voice as the nurse handed him Jack's chart. He began flipping through it and making some marks with a pen.

"On the third time, we barely got his heart working again," he continued, handing the chart back to the nurse. He looked back at Jack's bed and shook his head again. "Better keep a close watch on him tonight," he told the nurse, who nodded in agreement.

"Absolutely, doctor."

"I'm going to take a break, but call me if anything happens," Dr. Kelly said, and with that he left the room.

The nurse went back to typing information on the computer, unaware of the two spirits who had never left Jack. They were each on one side of the room, still wrapped up in their endless conversation.

53

"It appears that Jack Krantz may pull through after all," the good spirit remarked blithely, and the evil spirit scowled. "Bad news for you. Good news for Jack. You were hoping he would die on the operating room table so he would spend eternity in hell, were you not? If only people knew how horrible hell really is," he added soberly.

"I was counting on it," returned the evil spirit savagely. "You and I both know that if Krantz had died during surgery I'd have had him for good. And *you* would have lost any chance of snatching him away from me. After all, hasn't God told them that each one of them will give an account of themselves to Him?"

"Yes, but Jack isn't gone yet. I think he is going to make it," the good spirit replied. "And then he *will* have the chance to change."

The evil spirit began to move impatiently back and forth past the good spirit who watched him with slight amusement, and moved further out of his way. The evil spirit rubbed his hands together in a fury of frustration.

"If only God had given us power to do other things to humans besides tempt them!" he muttered lividly to himself, his burning eyes darting back and forth. "So I could kill him now and take him with me. Right *now...*"

The evil spirit turned toward Jack with such hideous loathing on his face that if Jack could have seen him he would have certainly feared for his life.

"God has kept us both from outside help," said the good spirit, wishing he too could do something about Jack, but in a very different contrast to the evil spirit's intentions. "We have no power to physically intervene in the lives of humans."

"I know that!" the evil spirit snapped, gritting his teeth in furious frustration. "I hate them," he growled. He and the good spirit locked eyes in a battle of stares between purity and corruption.

"I hate them *all*," the evil spirit seethed, his eyes burning with so much hatred that fires appeared to be lit in his blood-colored pupils.

CHAPTER 7: JACK'S HEART

Just as the evil spirit finished speaking, Jack Krantz's heart stuttered, and stopped beating.

The attending nurse in the room called a "Code Blue!" and doctors and nurses rushed into the room with a crash cart. Through the mania of activity as the medical personnel crowded around Jack, the two spirits moved silently across the room to watch the proceedings. The evil spirit had quickly straightened up when Jack's heart stopped, and watched excitedly as the doctors crowded around Jack. The good spirit moved towards the head of the bed, his pure, glowing pupils burning with white fire.

"Come on, Jack," he whispered to himself. He leaned over the bed and stared intently into Jack's closed eyelids. "Don't let go of life yet. I know you're still in there."

Jack's mind was filling rapidly with strange scenes and thoughts that flickered in and out like dying flames. As the nerve endings in his brain began to fire, the twisted shards of a dream crept over him as he sank deeper into the darkness…

He dreamed that his spirit slowly rose up, leaving his body. He looked around, then seeing his own body on the bed, his eyes widened in surprise and alarm. As he hovered near the bed, Jack's spirit suddenly noticed the evil spirit by the window.

When the evil spirit saw Jack looking curiously at him, he grinned poisonously.

"We know God gives these humans their spirit at the time they are conceived, but I'm always amazed when I get to see as they die, their bodies give their spirits up to us...mostly to me," he added with a wicked chuckle.

Jack didn't like the look of this darkly clothed figure with his evil face and fiery red eyes that were staring hungrily at him.

"Who are you?" he asked the dark spirit.

The evil spirit gave him a nasty smile.

"I'm the one who's here waiting to take you to the 'next place'," he responded darkly.

"What 'next place'?" Jack demanded curiously. "I didn't know there *was* a 'next place'."

"Everyone knows in their heart of hearts that there is a 'next place', Jack. They may not want to admit it to themselves, but they know it exists. And you, my friend, are going there with me very shortly."

"How do you know my name?" Jack's spirit demanded. "I don't know you."

"But I know *you*, Jack Krantz. And you may not recognize me, but you and I have actually been quite close over the years. And now I'm here to bring you to a place especially for people just like you."

"Where is this place?" asked Jack nervously. "What's it like?"

The evil spirit drew himself up, his eyes alight with a frightening flame that made Jack draw back involuntarily.

"Jack, it's the kind of place in which *no* human would *ever* want to end up. You're going to a place called '*Torment*' – a place where evil disembodied spirits (such as yourself) await the Day of Judgment. And trust me, its name adequately describes what goes on there. It's a place of unspeakable evil, pain and punishment. A place of utmost darkness and fire."

The evil spirit spoke each word with relish, as though he savored the sound of the horrible words.

"Torment?" Jack's spirit moved farther away from the evil spirit. His wonder had turned to terror. "No. I don't want to go to such a place. And you can't *make* me!"

"You'll do exactly what I say," the evil spirit told him. "Because you'll have *no choice* in the matter! You see Jack, your choices have already been made as a result of your conduct while you lived. And it is those choices that have determined...you *will* go to Torment."

Jack's spirit shuddered as a fear he had never known before spread through him. He felt so vulnerable and helpless. Looking around in despair, he saw the second spirit standing near him.

"Who are *you*?" he asked with trepidation.

"I'm the one who would have taken you to a very different

place – a better place – if you had been qualified to go there," answered the good spirit sadly.

"A better place?" Jack's spirit exclaimed. "Where? What's it like?"

"It's a place called 'Paradise', Jack," the good spirit explained gently. "It's where the righteous disembodied spirits go to await the Judgment Day."

"Is it a good place, then?" Jack's spirit demanded eagerly. "A nice place?"

"Oh yes. But it isn't just 'good' – it's *perfect*. In fact, it is the most wonderful place imaginable. It is *beyond* the imaginable. In Paradise there is no pain, no sorrow, no suffering, no sadness, no–"

"I want to go there!" Jack interrupted loudly. "I don't want to go with *him*!" He pointed back at the evil spirit.

"I'm sorry, Jack," the good spirit told him sorrowfully. "But you made that decision during your lifetime by the actions you took and the choices you made. Now, it's too late. Only while you were living could that decision be altered. Once you have died, your ability to change where you are going is revoked. God gave you the information you needed to choose properly and wisely. But you, Jack, chose *unwisely*."

As the good spirit spoke, Jack's spirit grew more and more dejected, and his face changed to an expression of deadly fear. He looked back at the dark spirit grinning at him and was repulsed. He turned back to the good spirit, who was beginning to fade from view.

"No!" Jack cried in horror. "Wait...I didn't know...I didn't understand! I don't want to go with him! I want..."

Dr. Kelly for the third time applied the electric pads to Jack's chest in another desperate effort to get his heart beating again. Suddenly the heart monitor began to beep, indicating the restarting of Jack's heart with a strong, regular beat.

The doctor and nurses were all so relieved to see that Jack was back among the living. As the nurses began to clean

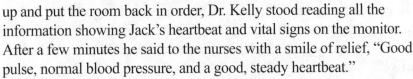

up and put the room back in order, Dr. Kelly stood reading all the information showing Jack's heartbeat and vital signs on the monitor. After a few minutes he said to the nurses with a smile of relief, "Good pulse, normal blood pressure, and a good, steady heartbeat."

To himself, Dr. Kelly thought, *This guy sure doesn't know how fortunate he is.* He didn't want to admit to himself that in that slim time frame between that last shock and Jack's heart restarting he had been afraid they would lose the patient.

One of the nurses interrupted his thinking.

"Doctor, should one of us stay with him?"

Dr. Kelly glanced at Jack's monitor once more, then shook his head.

"No, just continue to monitor him closely tonight and notify me if his condition worsens. I hope from here on out he'll remain stable. Alright everyone," he added loudly, bringing his hands together in a smart clap. "Let's clean up and leave so we can let him rest. I'll be back to see him in the morning."

In a few minutes, the nurses went out with the equipment, leaving the room dark except for a single night light above Jack's bed. Other than the soft sound of Jack's steady breathing and the constant low beeping of his heart monitor, the room was silent. Jack was alone now, for the two spirits had vanished, and the terror of the nightmare was shattered.

Elizabeth Emerson pushed her brother's wheelchair into one of the hospital elevators and stood silently behind him as they ascended several stories. Tyler sensed his sister's disapproval, but he didn't break into her sullen thoughts. The elevator doors opened onto a long hallway and Elizabeth began pushing Tyler's wheelchair along the corridor.

About halfway down, Elizabeth pulled up short just outside of the ICU doors.

"This is as far as I go, Tyler," she said firmly. "As you know, I didn't want to make this trip in the first place. The only reason I came was to drive you since you couldn't get here on your own."

Tyler lookcd pleadingly up at his sister.

"Elizabeth, please, don't be like that," he begged. "Come visit Jack with me."

"No, Tyler. *No!* I am *not* going to visit Jack Krantz and act as if everything is fine between us...because it's not!"

Tyler sighed. "I know, Lizzie, I know. But perhaps if *we* take the first step–if *we* are willing to go the extra mile–then maybe things *can* be fixed. And then things will be–"

"No, Tyler," Elizabeth repeated angrily. "Things will never be 'fine' between us and Jack. Never. There is nothing that you or I can say or do that will *ever* change Jack Krantz. And pardon me for saying so, but if he had died in the front yard the world would have been a whole lot better off."

"Lizzie, don't say such things. You know you don't really mean that."

"Yes, Tyler, I do!" Elizabeth suddenly exploded into a furious rant. "Jack's a liar, a swindler, an adulterer, a cheat, a scoundrel and a crook. There's not a decent bone in his entire body. He's not worth the bullet it would take to put him out of his misery!"

"That's enough!" said Tyler sternly. His sister looked at him in surprise. Usually Tyler was very mild-mannered. He rarely raised his voice.

He took a deep breath as he looked up at Elizabeth.

"Lizzie, you may not see anything good in Jack. But God does. And because you and I are Christians, God expects us to do likewise."

Elizabeth exhaled sharply, her arms folded while she glowered at the floor.

"We don't have a choice," Tyler explained patiently. "We have to try to help Jack."

Elizabeth was dumbfounded. "Help him? After all he's done to you? How do you plan to help him?"

"Lizzie, Jack is still alive. God has always provided the information people need to change their lives. And as long as Jack is still living he can access that information, learn from it, repent, and change."

Elizabeth snapped her head around to stare at her brother in shock. "Jack Krantz, *repent*?! You've got to be kidding!"

Tyler shook his head. "No Lizzie, I'm not. Remember that old saying, 'When you're flat on your back there's only one way you can look: *up*!' People can feel the need for God the most when their lives are in turmoil."

Elizabeth was pacing back and forth across the hallway, her arms still folded. Now she uncrossed them and ran her fingers agitatedly through her beautiful red hair.

"Jack's life has been in turmoil from the day he was born!" she cried. "He's had an entire lifetime to repent and he hasn't..."

Tyler shook his head, steadfastly refusing to accept her words. Elizabeth could see she wasn't moving him, and knelt down in front of his wheelchair. She looked her brother straight in the eyes.

"Give up, Tyler," she pleaded. "Jack isn't salvageable."

Elizabeth couldn't stand to watch her brother suffer any more over hopes he had built up only to watch them crash around him. She knew he wanted Jack to be saved, but she was also certain that Jack would not change. It hurt her to see her brother, so trusting, so hopeful, be disappointed so many times by the same man. She wanted Tyler to accept the truth: that Jack's heart would never change, and to move on and stop agonizing over it.

Tyler looked back into his sister's eyes. For one moment, she thought he might actually agree with her...

But then...

'"I don't believe that, Lizzie," he slowly shook his head again. Elizabeth sighed and bowed her head, knowing now that her brother truly would not change his mind.

"And neither should you!" Tyler went on earnestly. "No one – not even a man like Jack – is beyond God's reach. Remember King David and how he was forgiven for his terrible sins after he repented. Remember the words of the Bible spoken on God's behalf: 'I love those who love Me, and those who seek Me diligently will find Me.' If I could convince Jack to repent and seek God..."

"Tyler...Tyler, you're dreaming," Elizabeth sighed, almost laughing at how ridiculous the thought was. "Absolutely dreaming. It's not going to happen."

"But it could!" Tyler exclaimed. "How will we know unless we try? And I, for one, dear sister, am willing to try."

Elizabeth cracked a smile.

"Come with me," Tyler pleaded with her again. "I have to try again."

But his sister's face had hardened again.

"No," she said stonily. "You go. I want nothing more to do with Jack Krantz."

Realizing that she wasn't going to bend, Tyler turned his wheelchair away from her and began wheeling himself into the ICU alone. When he reached room 306 with the small name reading 'Krantz, Jack,' he took a deep breath and saw his hands were shaking. He was about to go speak to the man who had ruined his whole life and felt no remorse about it...and that same man now lay alone and friendless in a hospital bed recovering from a freak injury. Would he listen to anything Tyler had to say? Would he care at all that he had come?

Tyler steeled himself and, softly opening the door, he wheeled himself into the room. It was a private room, and the occupant lay sleeping on the bed. Tyler studied the thin, stony face of his old friend. Jack's good looks had been somewhat modified by the results of his accident and the surgery. His chiseled face was flecked with dark, unshaven stubble, and his closed eyes were ringed in dark purple. Lying on the bed, he seemed thinner than when Tyler had last seen him, and his already pale skin had an unhealthy pallid look. His breathing was even and regular, but his mouth was tightened as if he was agitated in his sleep.

Tyler could feel nothing but sympathy, even as he remembered the awful things this one-time friend had done to him. He wheeled himself quietly over to Jack's bedside. Carefully taking Jack's limp hand in his, Tyler bowed his head and began to pray.

"You have heard that it was said, 'You shall love your neighbor and hate your enemy.' But I say to you, love your enemies, bless those who curse you, do good to those who hate you, and pray for those who spitefully use you and persecute you,"   **-Matthew 5:43-44**

CHAPTER 8: TWO OLD FRIENDS

It was a stormy spring day. Sheets of cold rain were falling, and frequent peals of rolling thunder complete with occasional flashes of lightning scarred the heavy gray sky.

The Emersons' old Toyota pulled into the hospital parking lot as the rain drummed down. After they pulled into a parking spot, Elizabeth got out of the driver's seat wearing a heavy raincoat. Pulling the hood up over her head to keep off the rain, she hurried to the back of the car and opening the trunk, took out Tyler's wheelchair. She opened up the chair and rolled it around to the passenger door of the front seat, and opened the door so Tyler could get out. Her brother carefully maneuvered himself over from the car into his wheelchair while she held it steady for him.

"So," she remarked as Tyler settled into his wheelchair and wrapped his coat more tightly around himself. "I guess you're going to waste the…what is it now…sixth day in a row sitting with Jack again?"

"He may come around today," said Tyler briefly. "I want to be there for him and be able to talk to him when he wakes up."

Elizabeth just shook her head as she wiped raindrops out of her eyes, wondering how her brother could be so persistent about such a lost cause. At the same time Tyler was wishing Elizabeth would soften and feel some compassion for Jack, but he was sad to see she remained steadfastly set against the very existence of the man. Tyler opened his mouth to speak but Elizabeth quickly put up her hand to stop him, knowing full well what he was about to say.

"I've told you already. I'm not going in there," she said sternly. "Not today or any day. You shouldn't keep asking me."

Grieved, Tyler lowered his head. He understood it was useless talking to Elizabeth about this. Grabbing the big wheels on either side of his chair he began wheeling himself toward the hospital entrance doors. Suddenly he stopped, turned himself around and called back to his sister.

"Lizzie, at least pray for Jack, please?" he called through the rain.

Elizabeth, who had been getting back into the car, straightened back up and leaned on the door.

"Tyler," she said wearily, "I have to go find us a place to live, then go home and start packing. Call me when you want me to come pick you up."

With that, Elizabeth slammed the car door and drove off as a searing bolt of lightning lit up the dark gray sky overhead with a loud crack. Tyler turned himself back around and rolled into the hospital.

When Tyler entered Jack's room, Jack appeared to still be unconscious. Tyler wheeled himself softly over to the bed. As he had for the past several days, he picked up Jack's limp white hand from where it lay on the coverlet and began to pray silently for him. After a few seconds though, Jack began to stir. He moaned faintly and turned his head. As his dark eyes slowly opened, he looked up at the ceiling of the room, trying to bring his vision into focus.

"Ah, Jack, you're awake. How are you?"

Jack turned his head and saw Tyler Emerson sitting beside his bed. Though tired and weak, Jack's astonishment at seeing his visitor was enough to make his eyes grow suddenly wider, and he raised his head an inch off his pillow.

"Tyler...what are you doing here?"

The usual cold, arrogant tenor in his voice was gone, replaced by exhaustion, pain, and curiosity.

"I've been concerned about you ever since your accident on our front lawn, Jack," Tyler told him kindly. "The doctor said that your heart had stopped last week. I wanted to come see how you're doing."

Jack painfully shifted himself up into a half-upright position.

"I have to admit," he said thoughtfully, "I am surprised to find *you* sitting beside my bed. But then, I guess I shouldn't be."

Tyler winced, expecting another snide remark about his 'Christian principles.'

"During all the years that we were partners, you always tried to do what was right," Jack went on slowly. He looked down at his hands, fishing for the right words for what he wanted to say. Then he looked back at Tyler.

"I'm glad you decided to come see me," he said.

The genuine sincerity in Jack's voice startled Tyler. The haughty demeanor had dimmed profusely in contrast to their last meeting. Tyler hadn't seen such emotion in his old partner in several years. This filled him with hope.

"Jack, regardless of our differences through the years, I've always considered you as my friend," he said gently, noting the strange look Jack gave him. "I still do, in fact. When I heard that you almost died–"

"Almost?" Jack broke in with sudden energy. "The nurses told me I was 'technically dead' for a couple of minutes before the doctors revived me. Not a pleasant thought, eh?"

Tyler pursed his lips in an effort to choose his next words carefully.

"Jack," he began, "let's face it. We're *all* going to die. And when we do we're going to go through eternity in either Heaven or hell. But God doesn't want *anyone* going to hell. The Bible teaches us that God takes no pleasure in the death of the wicked. He wants everyone to go to Heaven. And that's what He wants for you."

Jack sat silently, digesting Tyler's words. Tyler couldn't see what was going on behind that impassive face, but he didn't have to wait long to find out.

"Well...I admit that as I've laid here in this bed, I've had some time to think about matters of life and death and–"

"Jack," Tyler broke in urgently, "I've tried to discuss these things with you before and every time I did, you ignored me. I hope this time you'll stop and seriously consider the things I've said to you in the past."

Jack bit his lips. He looked at the IV needle in his hand for a few seconds in a moody silence. Outside, the storm had grown steadily worse and the heavy rain beating against the window had turned the world on the other side of the glass into a watery blur. Other than the sound of the rain hitting the roof there was no sound between the two men.

Then...

"Okay," Jack said. "I'm listening. But Tyler, let me ask you a question."

"Sure," Tyler said, thrilled that Jack was actually interested in what he was trying to tell him.

"Do you think each of us has a spirit in us that we can't see?" asked Jack, looking down at the bed cover as he rolled it back and forth in his hands.

"Jack," said Tyler, "you know it really doesn't matter what I believe, only what God said. He has told us there is a spirit living inside every one of us that lives throughout this life and goes on to live after we die. I have told you this before, remember?"

Jack nodded, getting the answer he was looking for.

"It's just..." he said slowly, "I had this really bizarre dream the other night..."

Jack kept twisting the sheet into a tight roll, staring down at his hands. Confused and curious, Tyler watched him, unsure where Jack's words were leading them. Jack looked seriously troubled, and seemed reluctant to go on about the dream.

"Is there really a place like hell, Tyler? Is it real?" Jack finally looked up at Tyler, and Tyler couldn't help feeling a little intrigued by the genuinely concerned and curious emotions flickering across Jack's face. Tyler had never seen Jack Krantz like this before: in a somber frame of mind, in a mood when he really wanted to know about spiritual matters. He had always blown off that type of conversation in the past.

"Again, Jack, God has also said there is not only a place called hell – a place of everlasting torment, suffering and eternal darkness – but He has also told us there is a very wonderful place called Heaven. That's where the spirits of those who are faithful followers of God's Son Jesus Christ will live on forever."

Jack listened with rapt attention to Tyler's words as they sunk into his mind. Tyler's verbal illustration of hell made Jack's blood run cold. He thought he wouldn't ever need to see it to know he didn't want to go there.

"Jack, let me ask you something," said Tyler carefully. Jack turned his head expectantly toward him.

"What do you think would have happened to you the other night if the doctors hadn't been able to restart your heart again? And where do you think *your* spirit would have gone after your death – Heaven or hell?"

Jack sat very quietly. Tyler did not push him for an immediate answer. He knew Jack was a very smart man and, if he was completely honest with himself, would have to admit the truth.

"If I were to die right now..." Jack said suddenly. "My spirit would go to hell."

A crack of thunder boomed loudly right outside the window.

"Jack," Tyler's voice was gentle. "You know that doesn't have to happen."

"What do you mean, it 'doesn't have to happen'?" demanded Jack in surprise. His heart had sunk at the self-realization that he was condemned, but Tyler made it seem like there was a way of escape from his terrible fate.

"First, no one *has* to go to hell, Jack," said Tyler earnestly. "God wants everyone to go to Heaven, but He doesn't force anyone to go. The choice is yours. But the only people going to Heaven must be faithful Christians. And there in Heaven their spirits will live forever with God, Jesus His Son, God's Spirit and all the saints and angels that will be there. God made a point to tell us that no one else will be in Heaven."

Jack knit his brows in deep thought.

"And what do you mean by 'faithful' Christians?" he asked.

"Well, a lot of people *say* they are Christians but they do not live according to the commandments of Jesus Christ. Instead they keep living in sin."

Jack looked at Tyler with a queer expression.

"How do you know all this?" he wondered aloud.

Tyler reached into one of the pockets inside his coat and pulled out a worn black Bible. He held it up to Jack.

"God has told us this and much more through His Word, Jack. And He has told us we need to study it to know the Truth, for the Truth will make us free."

Determined to tell his old friend about the knowledge that had changed his own life, Tyler leaned forward as he began to explain to Jack the words of God.

"Jack, God loves you. He loves you so much that He was willing to send His Son to earth to die so you could go to heaven when *you* die. Neither of us wants to die, Jack, only to discover that we've ended up in a place so horrible that the human mind can't even conceive of the terror that exists there. Have you ever thought about that?"

Jack, fidgeting with the cover on his bed, suddenly grew very still. His expression was more serious than Tyler had seen it in a long time.

"Tyler..." he said very slowly, still turning the thought over in his mind as he struggled for the right words. "Suppose I *did* want to do something to avoid ending up in hell? What, exactly, would I have to do?"

Tyler smiled.

"Jack, there's nothing at all complicated about becoming a Christian and avoiding hell. God has provided a simple plan that can be easily understood and followed. Here, let me outline it for you."

"Okay."

"First, of course, you have to believe God exists and that Jesus is His Son. And you can do that! There is ample evidence to prove God's existence and to establish that Christ is Who He claimed to be," Tyler explained earnestly. He was watching Jack's face the entire time, joyful at the interest that God's Word seemed to have sparked in the other man.

"If I was to develop an...interest...in pursuing this..." said Jack, "could you show me some of that evidence?"

"Of course I could, and I would be happy to do so!" Tyler said. "Once you've seen it, there won't be any doubt in your mind about who Jesus is. And that knowledge will then lead you to the second step: repentance."

Here comes the hard part, thought Tyler uneasily. But he was determined.

"Jack," he said as kindly as he could, "you *have* to repent of your evil ways – of the type of lifestyle you've lived ever since I've known you. You need to live the way God wants you to live – not the way *you* want to live."

Tyler kept watching Jack's face carefully. He saw the eyes flash in the face of his old partner and feared his help would be thrown away unwanted at this point. For a minute he could see some of the cold, hard Jack Krantz he knew.

And then Jack exhaled, and the fire faded from his eyes.

"Okay," he began, "for the sake of argument, say I *was* willing to repent and change the way I live. Then what?"

Jack turned to stare out the window, and his voice dropped to a low murmur of...was it regret? "I've done a lot of bad things in my life, Tyler. Some *really* bad things. And...and I'm not proud of them...not anymore. Can God really forgive me for those sins?"

Tyler could hardly believe his ears. He leaned forward in his wheelchair, desperately eager to convince Jack that he was on the right track.

"Jack, God can and is very willing to forgive you," he said with earnestness. "Let me tell you about two men whom God forgave for some pretty awful sins. One man's name was David. He committed adultery and to hide it he lied and had the woman's husband killed."

Jack bit his lips, and Tyler suddenly felt his throat tightening up. But neither man told the other he was thinking about

Rachel Emerson.

Tyler cleared his throat and went on, pushing his emotions aside. He knew this was more important than what had happened in the past.

"Later, David repented of his sin and asked God to forgive him. God did punish David, because sin carries consequences, but God also forgave David."

"Wow," Jack remarked. "So David was forgiven and he could just start over fresh?"

"Absolutely. God wipes our sins away when, as Christians, we truly repent. God even forgets about our sins after we repent, Jack. And He loves us enough to keep forgiving us even when we keep sinning and have to keep asking for forgiveness."

The incredulity and wonder on Jack's face caused Tyler to hide a smile as he talked to his old partner about God's love. "But let me tell you about the other man God forgave," he added quickly, rustling through the pages of the Bible on his lap. "His name was Paul. Paul did everything he could to hurt, imprison and even kill those who followed Jesus. He thought what he was doing was right, but later he understood that he was doing wrong, and even called himself the chief sinner. God forgave him. Both these men, David and Paul, changed their lives when they realized they had sinned. Jack, God is always willing and ready to forgive us if we truly repent and in our hearts determine never to commit those sins again."

"So..." said Jack slowly, "if I believe in Jesus that He's God's son and I repent, then I'm good to go?"

"Jack, it's not enough just to believe Jesus is the Son of God. You've got to be willing to confess that fact to others – with your own lips. But remember this: once *you* come to truly believe it, confessing it will not only be easy, but joyous."

Jack cocked his head. "Is that it?"

"No, Jack," said Tyler. "There are two other things you must do."

"Which are?"

"In order to get rid of your sins you must be baptized. When Christ's church first began almost two thousand years ago, people asked what they needed to do to be saved and they were told: 'Repent, and let every one of you be baptized in the name of Jesus Christ for the remission of sins.' The Bible teaches us that this is *when* and *where* we come into contact with Christ's blood – the only thing that can wash away our sins," said Tyler.

Jack's face hardened.

"I'm in no position to do that right now – even if I wanted to," he said curtly. "It's just not do-able."

"Yes, Jack, it *is* do-able!" Tyler exclaimed. "I'm willing to help you, even while you're in the hospital. Others have done it under similar circumstances. So can you!"

"But you said there were *two* other things I had to do," Jack pressed him. "That's one. What's the second?"

Tyler smiled.

"When you are baptized, Jack, you are saved. God has taken away all of your sins. Now, it's up to you to *live like it* and try not to sin in the future. From the moment you step out of that water, you begin living like God wants you to live. He doesn't ask any more of you than that and He won't accept any less! God *wants* us to be saved and to live with Him forever in Heaven when we die."

Jack uttered a short laugh. "Well one thing's for sure. If a guy believed in hell, he sure wouldn't want to go there!"

Then his fine, dark eyebrows wrinkled in thought as he grew more serious again.

"I'm just not sure I–" he began, but Tyler cut him off.

"Jack, you and I have been over all of this before. This isn't the first time we've discussed these things," he repeated impatiently. "You *know* God exists. You *know* Christ is His Son. You *know* what you have to do to be saved. And you *know* there is a hell – where you *don't* want to go! The question is: are you going to act on this knowledge? Say the word, Jack, and I'll do whatever it takes to help you – right here, right now."

Jack leaned his head back against the pillow and closed his eyes. He seemed about to speak, then remained silent. The clock ticked softly on the wall. Tyler waited.

"I want to be saved," Jack said, breaking the tense silence at last. He looked at Tyler and his dark eyes were moist, though he kept his voice firm. "I don't want to be lost in hell. What can I do?"

"If you repent Jack, which you have, and believe Jesus is God's Son, which you do, all that's left is to baptize you for the forgiveness of your sins," Tyler answered. He was filled with joy that the man who had been against Christianity and morality for so long could finally see the truth that he so desperately needed to change his life. It showed the power of God's Word could transform the worst of men.

"How can I do that?" Jack asked soberly.

"I can see about making arrangements for your baptism here in the hospital," Tyler offered.

"What do you mean?" Jack asked again.

"All we need is a large enough space so you can be completely immersed under water," Tyler said.

"Well...wouldn't it be easier to just sprinkle some holy water on me or something? I'm not really in a position to be put completely underwater, Tyler. Or maybe you could just pour a little water over my head? Wouldn't that work?" Jack questioned.

"Those aren't real baptisms as God teaches us in the Bible, Jack. They don't count," Tyler explained patiently. "You have to be covered by the water – completely covered, every part of you – in your baptism."

"Why? Sorry, I just don't quite understand why I have to be completely covered in the water," Jack said uncomfortably.

"That's understandable Jack. And I'll tell you why: when you're baptized you are re-enacting the death, burial, and resurrection of Jesus Christ. You die to sin and self, as Jesus died on the cross. Then you are buried in the waters of baptism, as Jesus was buried in the tomb. Then you come up out of the waters of baptism a new Christian, as Jesus was raised from the dead and went up into Heaven and reigns at the right hand of God."

Jack thought about that for a while, taking in everything Tyler had just said. Finally, he slowly nodded in understanding.

"Yes, Tyler. That makes sense."

The door opened, and Dr. Kelly entered the room.

"How are you feeling this morning, Mr. Krantz?" he asked warmly as he took a look at the heart monitor.

"Much better than yesterday, thanks," Jack responded.

"Well that's great to hear!" the young doctor smiled and checked Jack's chart.

Jack glanced at Tyler. Tyler spoke up.

"Doctor, is it possible to arrange a baptism of immersion for Jack today?" he asked.

Dr. Kelly turned around, and at the look of unwilling concern on his face, Tyler knew his answer before he spoke.

"I'm sorry, sir, but at this point I don't think that would be wise. Mr. Krantz still has a drain tube in his chest and it would be too risky to put him underwater. I would give him about three more days," he said. Dr. Kelly's tone was pleasant and apologetic, but his words only made Tyler uneasy. He turned back to Jack.

"Gentlemen," Dr. Kelly nodded to both of them as he exited the room.

"Well, I guess we'll have to wait," said Jack uneasily.

"Yes, we don't have a choice," Tyler sighed.

"But Tyler, surely a few days won't make much difference. I mean, I'll be here in the hospital the whole time. What could happen to me?" Jack said. Tyler's gloomy expression made him nervous, and he wanted some words of comfort that he would be all right.

Tyler shook his head, disappointed.

"But if anything happens to you before you're baptized, Jack, you would still be lost because you haven't been completely converted. I wish we could take care of it right now, but that just isn't possible."

"Yes..." Jack frowned. "I really do want to be baptized,

Tyler. We just have to wait a few days, okay?"

Tyler nodded.

"I'll come back to see you again, Jack," he promised. "And here...I'll leave my Bible with you..."

"Will you come every day?"

Tyler hid a smile as he put his Bible carefully on Jack's nightstand. He never thought he would hear something like that from his old friend again. Perhaps the scattered, ruined threads of their long lost friendship could still be gradually collected, one at a time.

"Yes I'll come see you every day while you are in the hospital. We can study the Bible and pray. Would you like me to offer a prayer right now?"

Jack nodded gratefully, and the two men bowed their heads. When Tyler finished the prayer, Jack asked,

"Will you do me a big favor and call my office for me? I haven't had a chance to contact them yet. They won't know what happened to me."

Tyler promised to do this, and then held out his hand. Jack looked at it for a second, then hesitantly reached out, and he and Tyler exchanged a firm, friendly handshake.

When Tyler had wheeled himself out into the hall and called Elizabeth to come get him, he wheeled into an elevator and went down to the first floor. He waited in the lobby until he saw his sister come in through the front doors. Her first greetings to him were quite in harmony to the stormy day.

"Well, did your *friend* decide he wants to give you back your land and become a Christian today?" she asked sarcastically when she saw his big smile. She wondered what could have possibly occurred in his visit with Jack that could put such a happy look on his face.

"He didn't get that far," said Tyler, tactfully ignoring her cynicism as she got behind him to push his wheelchair out the door. "But at least he was willing to listen to the Gospel. And he does want to become a Christian!" he added elatedly.

Elizabeth pulled up short, stopping the wheelchair so suddenly that Tyler's head jerked forward and then back.

"Jack Krantz...wants to be a...*Christian*?! What in the world did you say to him?"

"I just told him about God's Word and what it takes to become a follower of Christ. I believe he really is earnest about becoming a child of God, Lizzie."

Tyler couldn't stop smiling. He was overjoyed that his old friend finally wanted to obey Christ.

"Well," remarked Elizabeth, somewhat at a loss for words as she pushed her brother's wheelchair out to the car, "I'm shocked. I never thought he had it in him to change. Are you sure he's not putting you on? Although he wouldn't have anything to gain really, I guess..."

Tyler didn't answer. He was deep in thought and prayer.

Jack is so close. So close... he thought to himself. *I hope he recovers quickly so he can be baptized as soon as possible. I wish he hadn't waited this long...*

The storm had eased up enough so that the thunder was only a faint rumble in the distance, and the rain was lighter as it drizzled down.

"And the Lord said, 'Simon, Simon! Indeed, Satan has asked for you, that he may sift you as wheat.'"   **-Luke 22:31**

"Excuse me, what is Jack Krantz's room number?"

Judith Miller stood at the information counter holding a small vase of flowers. When the receptionist there gave her the room number she walked down the hall to Jack's room. The door was open, and she knocked tentatively.

"Come in," Jack called out.

Judith entered the room and set the vase of flowers on Jack's bedside table. He looked pleased to see her, and carefully set aside the worn black book he had been reading.

"Judith, it's nice of you to come," he said politely. "Please, sit down."

His secretary pulled up a chair and sat down near the head of the bed.

"It's nice to see you looking so well after your accident, Mr. Krantz," she said carefully. "Mr. Emerson called last night to tell me what had happened and that you were in the hospital."

"Yes, it's been quite a ride!" Jack answered. "I know one thing for sure: I'll be a lot more careful in the future about where I step when I'm around garden rakes!" He winced as he remembered the agony of the sharp spikes sinking into his back.

Judith nodded understandingly. "Mr. Emerson didn't give me very many details when he called. He said you had been in a serious accident. What exactly happened?"

"Yes. I had walked out the front door of the house where the Emersons are living. As I stepped down off the porch, either one of the boards broke or I lost my footing – I'm not quite sure which. I remember losing my balance and starting to fall. I tried to catch myself, but I guess I wasn't very successful, huh?" Jack smiled humorlessly "The next thing I knew, I woke up in the hospital's emergency room with a rake sticking out of my back!"

"Oh Mr. Krantz, that sounds horrible!" cried Judith, putting her hand over her heart. "Mr. Emerson said you had to have open-heart surgery!"

"Yes, I did. The surgery, so I understand, went just fine. But after I had been moved into intensive care something happened that caused my heart to stop. The doctors told me that I was 'technically dead' for a very brief period."

Judith marveled at the calm manner in which Jack could speak about his own death, however shortly it had lasted. Dead is dead, after all, no matter how long a time.

"I can't believe this, Mr. Krantz!" she exclaimed. "I just can't believe it! You leave the office on a business matter and just disappear for days with none of us at the office knowing what happened, and then the next thing I know, I'm getting a call from your former partner telling me that you're in the hospital and it had been a life or death situation."

"I know," Jack replied soberly. "It's been a pretty scary time all the way around. Nothing I'd ever like to repeat, that's for sure."

"Well, I'm certainly glad to see that you're feeling better and that you're healing," Judith told him. "Also, I didn't come by just to say hello. I wanted to find out if there is some way I can help."

Jack smiled appreciatively.

"Is there something I can do for you – either at the office or for you personally?" Judith offered.

"Nice of you to ask, Judith," Jack answered sincerely. "And as a matter of fact...yes. There are a few things I would like you to take care of for me, if you don't mind."

Judith had not witnessed her boss being this polite in a long time, if ever. His relaxed and more considerate attitude put her off guard.

Maybe it's the pain medication, she thought.

"Certainly," she said aloud, trying to keep the surprise out of her voice. "What do you need me to do?"

She reached into her purse and pulled out a small pad of paper and a pen to take notes.

"If you could go by my house every day or so and get

the mail from my mailbox until I'm able to go home, I would appreciate it," Jack began, and Judith scribbled hastily on her notepad.

"Also, if you would pick up the newspapers off the porch, it would be a big help," Jack continued. "That way, people will think there's someone at home."

Judith finished scribbling with a flourish.

"Not a problem. I'll run by your house as soon as I leave here and pick up the mail and newspapers from the last few days," she promised, and Jack nodded his thanks. "What else can I do?"

Jack's brow wrinkled in thought.

"I think that everything else at the house will be just fine," he mused. "However, there are a couple of things I need you to do around the office."

"I'll write down whatever you need done to be sure it gets taken care of," Judith said eagerly. She was anxious to please her boss when he was in a nice frame of mind, and make him as easy in his mind as possible after the harrowing accident he had just gone through.

"First," and Jack, sat up a little more and resumed some of his businessman-like attitude, "bring me a new cell phone, would you? I lost mine somewhere between now and last Friday. As for the office, make sure the interns are kept busy on their assignments. I had given them enough to do to keep them busy for several days, but I don't want them goofing off. Stay on top of them for me, okay?"

"I can do that," Judith answered proudly. "And I'll let everyone in the office know what's happened to you and that you'll be back before long."

Jack smiled approvingly. "Good. Be sure to keep track of my phone messages and call me if something needs handling. I'll need to return people's calls once I get out of here. Tell them I hope – no, *plan* to be back at work next week."

"Yes sir." Judith flipped the page on her notepad and continued writing furiously. "Right now, so far as I know, there's

79

nothing pressing at the office." She bit her lip and looked upwards for a second, tapping her pen against her notepad and trying to think. "We don't have any real estate closings happening anytime soon...I think the nearest one is about two weeks away, so that shouldn't present any problems."

"No, I'll be out of here by then," said Jack confidently. "I should be able to take care of the closings on my own. In the meantime," he added, "make sure to deliver to the newspaper all the information for our new listings. I want them to appear in the weekend edition. I think the deadline for getting them in is in a couple of days."

"Alright..." The movement of Judith's pen on paper filled the pause. "I'll assign that to one of the interns. Anything else?"

"That's about all I can think of for now," said Jack. "I'll let you know if I think of anything else."

"Yes, sir." Judith slipped her notepad and pen back into her purse. "Have they told you how long you're going to have to stay in the hospital?"

"No, my doctor hasn't said anything about that. But it shouldn't be too much longer."

Jack's voice was hard and he looked determined to be out of the hospital and on his way back to work very soon. Knowing her boss well, Judith knew the inactivity was eating at him.

"Well, the sooner the better," she said cheerfully. "For now, let me get going so that I can take care of these things."

Jack nodded and Judith stood up.

"Oh, and Judith," Jack suddenly moved, then winced as his muscles pulled at the stitches in his body. "Remember to get me a phone."

Judith grinned and patted her outside purse pocket containing the notepad with Jack's list.

"It's all right here. I won't forget," she said. "I'll bring it first thing tomorrow morning."

"Great," Jack said as she turned to go. "And by the way, thanks for the flowers."

CHAPTER 9: "3:00 P.M. TODAY!"

Judith smiled. "I'm glad you like them."

She was almost to the door when she paused. She turned on the spot and hurried back to Jack.

"I almost forgot!" she said, pulling a large manila envelope out of her purse and holding it up.

Jack looked up at her questioningly.

"The eviction papers you asked me to prepare regarding the Emersons have to be delivered to the courthouse today before three o'clock or we'll miss the deadline to file. After that, the eviction notice can't be served for ninety days."

Comprehension dawned on Jack's face. He studied the envelope in Judith's hand, saying nothing.

"Oh, and Senator Watson voted yes and the bill passed to have the government purchase your land for 80,000,000 dollars," Judith added as a newly-remembered afterthought.

Jack felt his face flush.

Keith did his job, he thought. He remembered the picture in the envelope and the disgusted look on his intern's face when Jack had told him to use it to push their agenda on the senator. Jack cringed when he thought regretfully about the offhanded way he had used bribery and blackmail to get what he wanted.

"Do you want me to take the papers to the courthouse, or ask one of the interns to do it?" asked Judith, wondering why he wasn't saying anything. When Jack had asked her to prepare the papers several days ago, he had been adamant in stressing the importance of the job. Now he looked...undecided, and almost unwilling.

"No," Jack said suddenly. "Don't do either one, Judith. Just leave the papers here on the table. I'll let you know what we need to do."

"Okay..." Judith laid the envelope on the little table beside the bed within Jack's reach. "You can reach me at the office. Oh, after I get you a phone, that is. Just remember that the papers have to be at the courthouse before three o'clock this afternoon," she warned as she walked out of the room, leaving Jack staring down

81

at the manila envelope, his brow furrowed in thought.

A few minutes after Judith left, Jack's physician, Dr. Kelly, came into the room. He briefly examined Jack and discussed with him how serious his initial injuries were.

"The nurse will be in shortly to remove the chest tube drain," explained the doctor, "You should be able to rest better tonight." Just before he left the room he gave Jack one last warning.

"You need a *lot* of rest, Mr. Krantz. Too much strenuous activity will reopen those stitches in your heart. You need to be still as much as possible so you can heal and regain your strength," Dr. Kelly told him. Jack reluctantly agreed, and the doctor pulled open the door to leave.

"If all goes well," he called back over his shoulder, "you should be able to go home in three or four days."

Dr. Kelly started to close the door behind himself, but then stopped. A thoughtful look came over his face and he walked back into the room. Jack turned to look at him curiously, wondering why he came back.

"You were the man who wanted to be baptized, is that correct, sir?" Dr. Kelly asked him.

Jack gave him a small smile. "Yes I am. But you said that at this point it's too much of a risk."

"Well, that's true." Dr. Kelly nodded. "But I think when that tube is out, in just a few days we can take care of it. I know this must be important to you."

Jack stared up at the doctor. "You do?"

"Yes, and I just wanted to let you know I'll do what I can to help speed your recovery so the baptism can happen," Dr. Kelly promised. Jack smiled gratefully.

"Thanks, doctor."

"Well, I'll let you rest. You need it. Don't do anything to wear yourself out," Dr. Kelly added the last sentence in a joking manner as he went back to the door. Once more, he turned to look at Jack.

"I'll be praying for you."

Jack's eyes widened in surprise and then gladness spread through him. He hadn't known Dr. Kelly was a Christian. The idea just hadn't occurred to him.

The door closed behind the doctor and Jack was again left alone. The silence was almost unnerving. He felt so tired but he was afraid to shut his eyes.

What if I die in my sleep? he thought anxiously. Forcing his eyes to stay open, Jack stared up at the ceiling. Then slowly his eyes traveled along the top of the walls around the room, idly taking in the plain white walls that had surrounded him for the past few days. He looked out the window where the storm had given way at last and the sun was shining warmly. Then his gaze came to a stop and rested on the clock.

12:15 P.M.

Jack studied the clock for a minute, then he looked down at the envelope on his bedside table. Judith had stuck a Post-It note on the outside of the envelope, and when Jack picked it up, he could read the message scribbled in black ink: **MUST BE DELIVERED TO COURTHOUSE BEFORE 3:00 P.M. TODAY!**

Jack held the envelope in his hand and studied it, a thoughtful expression on his face. What he held in his hand would remove the last obstacle standing between him and a goal that would make for him the deal of a lifetime. Here was the chance for which he had been waiting. He would profit so much from handing in these eviction papers...

Suddenly the words floated through his mind from a conversation days before...

"Jack...I've always considered you as my friend. I still do."

Why?

Jack couldn't understand why Tyler Emerson would still care about him after everything he had done to ruin his former partner's life. Jack Krantz had done his best to crush the Emerson's lives under his expensive shoes, and he had held them in the highest contempt. He hadn't always been intentionally trying to hurt them, he was just out to get what he wanted, and selfishly disregarded the lives of others in the process as long as he won in the end. But Tyler was still willing to look past their 'differences' (as he had so mildly put it) and hold out his hand in friendship to Jack, even if that hand was so often refused.

He's probably the only person who really cares about me and my soul, thought Jack, bothered by his strangely conflicted feelings. *What's wrong with him? No matter what I do, Tyler still tries to be my friend and be at peace with everyone.*

Jack couldn't decide if he admired this or was irritated by it.

He turned the envelope over and over in his hands, deliberating. He was surprised at himself that he was hanging between two choices: to hand in the papers and destroy a life, or let it all go. *This shouldn't be an issue.*

Jack sat still, just staring at the envelope. Then suddenly he tossed it into the trash can beside his bed. Closing his eyes he leaned back on his pillow, his face smooth and peaceful.

"Put on the whole armor of God, that you may be able to stand against the wiles of the devil."
-Ephesians 6:11

CHAPTER 10:
"HE APPEARED OUT OF NOWHERE"

The clock ticked away on the wall. The curtains were pulled back from the window to let in the warmth of the sunshine. All was quiet in the hospital room.

Waking from sleep, Jack's eyes snapped open. He began to look around the room as if not sure where he was. Seeing the clock on the wall he began to stare at it as if trying to remember that there was something important regarding time. Suddenly, he sat up in bed with a strange look on his face, and threw back the sheet and blanket covering him. Swinging his legs over the side and sitting on the edge of the bed, he unplugged the plastic tubing from the IV inserted in the back of his hand. The effort to rise made him inhale sharply as pain struck him deep inside his chest, and he pressed his hand against his wound. He limped painfully to the closet where he retrieved his clothes and shoes.

Just sliding his arms into the coat sleeves was agony, and for a minute Jack had to sit back down on the bed, holding his chest and breathing hard. Sweat stood out on his forehead, but he finished dressing and walked slowly back over to the trash can next to his bed. For about five seconds he looked down into it, then reached down and pulled out the large brown envelope.

It was 2:30 P.M. No time for anyone from the office to take care of this. Jack would have to do it himself. The thought of 80,000,000 dollars overcame the pain. All good reasoning left him; 80,000,000 dollars would provide him with more power and riches, everything he always wanted.

Jack made his way down the hospital hallway, avoiding the doctors and nurses. Reaching the elevator, he pressed the 'down' button with a shaking finger. It wasn't until after the elevator doors closed between him and the hallway that he sank back against the wall in the corner of the elevator, leaning his head back and trying to breathe without gasping. He wiped his sweaty forehead with the back of his hand. The burning in his chest was consuming him.

I can and must do this, he thought doggedly.

The elevator door opened at the ground floor. Jack made his way across the lobby and out the front doors of the hospital. A couple of taxis were waiting on standby outside the hospital doors, and Jack stumbled over to one. He slid into the back seat and with a groan managed to lean forward far enough to tell the driver, "Take me to the courthouse!"

The taxi driver turned his head at the ragged sound in Jack's voice.

"Hey fella, are you okay?" he asked curiously.

"Just take me to the courthouse," Jack repeated, sinking back against the seat and staring out the window.

As the taxi began moving forward through the busy streets of the city, Jack slumped in the back seat, glancing at his watch every few minutes. Intense concern crept over his face as he watched the time speeding away from him, moving ever closer to the three o'clock deadline. The time to file the papers in the envelope clutched against his chest was rapidly approaching faster than his taxi was moving. Jack almost forgot his pain in his frenzy of anxiety.

Then the taxi came to a stop.

"What's going on? Why are we stopping?" Jack demanded, alarmed. His words were disjointed as he struggled to catch his breath.

"I'm sorry sir, but this is as close as I can get. There's too much street construction in front of the courthouse," the taxi driver explained.

"What!"

Jack looked out the window and had to admit to himself that the taxi driver was right. Just ahead, the courthouse loomed high in front of him. But between the taxi and the courthouse almost the entire street was blockaded with construction workers, trucks, and equipment. Jack couldn't believe all this was impeding his important errand. This couldn't keep him from getting to the courthouse, it just couldn't.

The taxi driver was looking at him expectantly.

"I'll get out here!" said Jack in a strained voice.

CHAPTER 10:
"HE APPEARED OUT OF NOWHERE"

He dug out a couple of bills from his pocket and tossed them over the seat, looking at his watch as he did so. "Wait here. I'll be back in twenty minutes."

2:50 P.M.

He had ten minutes left. Jack opened the taxi door and stumbled out. Still holding the envelope tightly to his chest, he hurried down the sidewalk parallel to the construction site. The pain in his chest was almost too much for him, but it was the thought of getting the papers in before the deadline that kept him from crumpling to the ground. The courthouse stood in the middle of the town square, and Jack would have to cross the construction area to reach the courthouse.

He paused on the sidewalk across the street from the courthouse for just a moment to check his watch again. When he looked down, he saw little spots of blood seeping through his shirt. The stitches in his chest were broken, and his laceration had re-opened.

2:55 P.M.

Jack gritted his teeth and started across the street between two gravel trucks that were pulled up next to the curb. He looked down at his watch one last time, his panic rising when he saw how little time he had left.

Just as he was stepping out into the street from between the two gravel trucks, Jack was hit by a cement truck whose driver saw him too late to stop. Jack was thrown forward as the force of the vehicle slammed into him. The driver of the cement truck stopped and jumped out and rushed over, a look of horror on his face when he saw the man slumped on the ground.

"I didn't see him, he just appeared out of nowhere!"

Jack lay in the middle of the street, unconscious and bleeding profusely. Workers and other people on the courthouse square nearby rushed over to where he lay. A man pushed his way through the crowd, claiming he was a doctor and telling everyone to stand back. He knelt down beside Jack, checking his pulse and attempting to revive him.

87

But it was too late. Jack Krantz was dead. The doctor, realizing this, sat back on his heels and sadly shook his head. He could see there was already a large pool of blood beneath Jack's body. Wanting to cover the exposed face of the dead man, the doctor attempted to remove Jack's coat to cover the body, but then he saw that the dead man was holding a large brown envelope in his hand, preventing him from removing his coat completely. The doctor took the blood spotted envelope out of the dead man's hand and looked at it briefly before gently removing Jack's coat and spreading it over his lifeless face.

By this time a large crowd had huddled around the accident site, trying to get a glimpse of what had happened. Questions were raised as to the identity of the victim. When the doctor laid the coat over Jack and covered his face, everyone knew that whoever the man was, he was dead. The throng moved back and began to disperse.

As people moved about the area where the body lay, and as sirens began crying in the distance, no one saw the single solitary figure watching from across the street. No one saw the figure dressed all in black sitting on the hood of a parked car – right across from where the accident had taken place.

The spirit in black watched the activity across the street, his expression at first blank. But ever so slowly...the spirit's absent stare morphed into an insidious smile. And his eyes began glowing a bright, hellish red.

EPILOGUE

Elizabeth Emerson sat in the driver's seat of the car, reading to herself from her book while parked by the curb. Tyler had asked her to come with him again, but she had refused to leave the car. Her gaze drifted from her book for a minute as she looked out the window at her brother.

Tyler stood not far away from the car, surrounded by tombstones. But of all the graves in the cemetery around him his attention was focused solely on the one in front of him. The cold, black, granite headstone stood apart from the other graves. Large and ornate, it was larger than many of the tombstones in the cemetery, with the name Jack Krantz engraved on its surface in gold lettering.

Tyler stood looking at it for a few more seconds, his hands firmly gripping the handles of his new walker as he thought about what to say.

For he felt he should say something. After all, he and Jack had once been friends. And now that he and Elizabeth were moving away, this was the only chance he would have to say goodbye to his partner and friend. Even though Jack had treated him so poorly he remembered what the Lord said about doing good to those who do you harm.

"Well, Jack," he said softly to the gravestone, "I guess this is where we part ways. I always considered you my friend. I wish things could have been different between us, but it's too late for that now..."

Tyler struggled against the emotions rising inside him that forced a lump into his throat.

"You were so close," he whispered. "So close, Jack. If only you hadn't waited so long, I would feel so much better about where you are today. This could have turned out so differently. You could have been my brother."

Tyler took a deep breath, pinching his lips tightly together and blinking fiercely to hold back tears. Then he glanced around him at the other gravestones in the cemetery. He nodded to indicate to himself that he was finished here, and turning his walker slowly around he began moving back to the car.

Elizabeth helped him get into the car and closed up his walker so it could be stowed in the trunk. Then she got in and started the engine.

But instead of driving away, she sat still, both hands on the wheel of the car. Tyler looked at her, wondering why she just sat there.

"You know," she said reflectively, "I bet Jack Krantz would roll over in his grave if he knew he had forgotten to remove your name from the company insurance policy, leaving you everything in the case of his death."

Elizabeth turned toward her brother. Her bright blue eyes were thoughtful.

"Maybe you were right all along, Tyler," she said. He looked at her silently, an unvoiced question in his eyes. "God's justice always pays off in the end."

Tyler hung his head, wincing at her words.

"But look at the price Jack had to pay, Lizzie. The Lord has always taken care of us and I'm thankful for that, but it's not 'justice' or a 'pay off' if it costs a man his soul," he said wearily. He leaned his head back against the headrest of the seat as Elizabeth wordlessly put the vehicle in gear. As they drove away from the cemetery, Tyler looked over his shoulder toward Jack's grave one last time. A scripture he had heard countless times came to mind…

For what will it profit a man if he gains the whole world and loses his own soul?   *-Mark 8:36*

Jesus said…
"Enter by the narrow gate; for wide is the gate and broad is the way that leads to destruction, and there are many who go in by it. Because narrow is the gate and difficult is the way which leads to life, and there are few who find it."   *-Matthew 7:13-14*

"Then Jesus was led up by the Spirit into the wilderness to be tempted by the devil. And when He had fasted forty days and forty nights, afterward He was hungry. Now when the tempter came to Him, he said, 'If You are the Son of God, command that these stones become bread.' But He answered and said, 'It is written, 'Man shall not live by bread alone, but by every word that proceeds from the mouth of God.''

Then the devil took Him up into the holy city, set Him on the pinnacle of the temple, and said to Him, 'If You are the Son of God, throw Yourself down. For it is written: 'He shall give His angels charge over you,' and, 'In their hands they shall bear you up, Lest you dash your foot against a stone.''

Jesus said to him, 'It is written again, 'You shall not tempt the Lord your God.''

Again, the devil took Him up on an exceedingly high mountain, and showed Him all the kingdoms of the world and their glory. And he said to Him, 'All these things I will give You if You will fall down and worship me.'

Then Jesus said to him, 'Away with you, Satan! For it is written, 'You shall worship the Lord your God, and Him only you shall serve.'''

-Matthew 4:1-10

Then He will also say to those on the left hand, 'Depart from Me, you cursed, into the everlasting fire prepared for the devil and his angels:'"

-Matthew 25:41

Another Book from This Author

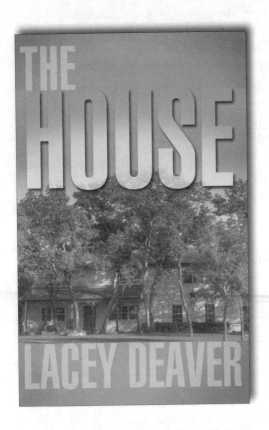

This story is an adaptation of the movie *Bound*, which won the Best Feature Film award in 2011.

BEST
FEATURE FILM
Seguin
Film Festival
2011

"The House" is a suspenseful story about love and doing good for others that will hold your interest until the very last page.

This Christian-fiction book is a full-color, 187-page, soft-cover printed version of the story used in the movie "Bound." The story is of a young woman whose life has been tormented with struggle and bad choices. A set of unforeseen circumstances finds her the reluctant guest of a family who helps her face the important decisions in her life. With her heart wounded by grief, unlikely friends come to her rescue, and with their help Cheri finds hope and learns the truth that will forever change her life.

Books from WVBS

–Searching for Truth Study Guides–

These study guides, written by **John Moore**, area great resource as a companion to the *Searching for Truth* DVD, or used on their own as a workbook. The material is suitable for individual study or used in any Bible class setting. the text follows the same chapter structure and is nearly a word-for-word transcript of the DVD.

The study guides include extended question sections, including a "Section Review" after each section and a "Chapter Review" at the end of each chapter. To close-out the chapter there is a "Digging Deeper" section, which includes additional verses on the subject matter that are not used in the text. The answer to every question can be found in the Answer Key section at the end of the book. Additionally, six teaching charts are included in the book. These 8.5 x 11 inch, full-color charts cover popular issues such as, "The Book of Daniel & God's Kingdom," "Where do we go when we die?," "Modern Churches Timeline," "The Ten Commandments?," Baptism's significance, and the Church as God's spiritual house.

English Study Guide

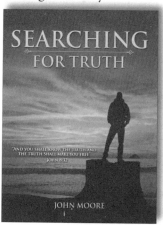

Spanish Study Guide

Over 120,000 printed!

Russian

Korean

Swahili

Available at www.wvbs.org
or call 512-398-5211

Books from WVBS

The TRUTH About
Moral Issues

This beautiful, 132-page, full-color, soft-cover book makes a wonderful teaching tool and gift for anyone who would like to study these subjects: Tattoos, Gambling, Drinking, Dancing, Lying, Modesty, Pornography, Marriage Divorce and Remarriage, and What Must I Do To Be Saved? These are lessons that everyone needs to study in order to understand how these topics could impact their lives spiritually and physically.

Books from WVBS

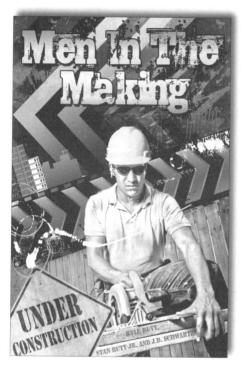

This full-color, 92-page soft-cover book provides a framework that helps every young man from 12 to 20 years old learn to honor the older, protect the weak, overcome sexual temptation, control their tongues, and stand for the Truth. This book is written by Kyle Butt, Stan Butt, Jr., and J.D. Schwartz.

Books from WVBS

Are you looking for a refreshing new book for ladies' class or personal study? Are you ready for an in-depth examination of portions of God's Word that you probably haven't studied before? This 106-page, soft-cover study book, *Songs of Deliverance*, considers the responses of God's people when He answered their prayers and delivered them from trials and tribulations. Stand amazed with the Israelites at the Red Sea as the waves swallow their enemies. Weep with Hannah and then learn the secret of her sacrifice. Look through David's time telescope and see Christ–and yourself! Through their songs, these Bible heroines and heroes reveal nuances of God's nature that will draw you closer to Him as you learn the joys and responsibilities of God's deliverance. Immerse yourself in the Songs of Deliverance, and your day will end on a good note.

Available at www.wvbs.org
or call 512-398-5211

Faith-Based Movie

BOUND

Bound to the world. Bound to man. Bound to God.

"A suspense filled, feel good movie. Loved it!"
-Don Blackwell *Gospel Broadcasting Network*

A moving story from loss and despair to help and hope. Bound, a story like no other, is about a young woman, Cheri Harper, whose life was filled with loss, struggle, despair, and bad choices. A set of unforeseen circumstances finds her the reluctant guest of a family who helps her face some very important decisions only to later believe she has been deceived. Unlikely friends come to her rescue and with their help she learns the truth and finds the hope that forever alters her life.

Stephanie Motal

Chad Motal

Al Washington

Rhonda Washington

Ferman Carpenter

Jean Carpenter

Ron Trotter

BEST FEATURE FILM Seguin Film Festival 2011

WORLD VIDEO BIBLE SCHOOL® PRESENTS "BOUND" STEPHANIE MOTAL CHAD MOTAL AL WASHINGTON RHONDA WASHINGTON FERMAN CARPENTER JEAN CARPENTER RON TROTTER MUSIC DAVID UNDERWOOD PHOTOGRAPHY & EDITING BY MAT CAIN WRITTEN & DIRECTED BY RUDY CAIN

Copyright © 2011
www.themoviebound.com
www.wvbs.org

| Run Time: 123 minutes | 16:9 Widescreen Presentation |
| Dolby Digital 2.0 | English Subtitles |

wvbs PICTURES

wvbs *School*

Serving the Church since 1986

Tuition-Free, 24/7, Online Bible School

World Video Bible School® is now offering a tuition-free, online Bible school. This school, including all Bible book courses and related curriculum, is accessible via the internet. The school curriculum is also available on DVD at a discounted price for students who cannot use the internet. The School is designed for use in the following ways:

- You can enroll as an audit-only student, taking as many or as few courses as desired to gain knowledge without any reading assignments, tests, memory work, or research papers. (No diploma or certificate awarded.)

- You can enroll as a student and follow an informal track, which means courses can be taken for your own learning and edification in any order with the associated memory work, reading assignments, tests, and research papers. (A certificate of completion will be awarded for each course.)

- You can enroll as a student and follow a formal track, which includes the completion of all memory work, reading assignments, tests, and research papers in the designated order and according to a specific level of proficiency. (A diploma will be awarded at completion of this program.)

- A congregation can operate their own school using WVBS instructors, syllabi, and related materials.

- Among the attractive points about this school is that it will be tuition-free, with the exception of necessary books and supplies. It also offers you an opportunity to study independently, 24/7, at your own pace and without the inconvenience of relocating. Additional information at:

school.wvbs.org

98